"Have you heard of unlucky Pierre?" Bartelmetz asked. "He was doing a dissertation on the evolution of consciousness. He decided it would be necessary to explore the mind of an ape, so he obtained illegal access to one of our Omnichannel Neural T & R Units. While his mind was linked with that of his hairy subject, something panicked the creature. Pierre is still residing in a padded cell, and all his responses are those of a frightened ape."

Render said, "I have nothing that dramatic to contend with—I'm simply using the ONT&R to guide a blind woman through the sight-trauma."

"But that is not simple at all," said Bartelmetz. "You are changing this woman's whole conception of herself and the world, and that can be very, very dangerous." He smiled sadly. "May the shades of Freud and Jung walk by your side in the valley of darkness," he said softly.

THE DREAM MASTER

ROGER ZELAZNY

SF
ace books

A Division of Charter Communications Inc.
A GROSSET & DUNLAP COMPANY
360 Park Avenue South
New York, New York 10010

To Judy,

of the hurst of oaks
with a wolf issuant therefrom
to the sinister all proper.
"Fidus et audax."

I

LOVELY AS it was, with the blood and all, Render could sense that it was about to end.

Therefore, each microsecond would be better off as a minute, he decided—and perhaps the temperature should be increased. . . . Somewhere, just at the periphery of everything, the darkness halted its constriction.

Something, like a crescendo of subliminal thunders, was arrested at one raging note. That note was a distillate of shame and pain, and fear.

The Forum was stifling.

Caesar cowered outside the frantic circle. His forearm covered his eyes but it could not stop the seeing, not this time.

The senators had no faces and their garments were spattered with blood. All their voices were like the cries of birds. With an inhuman frenzy they plunged their daggers into the fallen figure.

All, that is, but Render.

The pool of blood in which he stood continued to widen. His arm seemed to be rising and falling with a mechanical regularity and his throat might have been shaping bird-cries, but he was simultaneously apart from and part of the scene.

For he was Render, the Shaper.

Crouched, anguished and envious, Caesar wailed his protests.

"You have slain him! You have murdered Marcus Antonius—a blameless, useless fellow!"

Render turned to him, and the dagger in his hand was quite enormous and quite gory.

"Aye," said he.

The blade moved from side to side. Caesar, fascinated by the sharpened steel, swayed to the same rhythm.

"Why?" he cried. "Why?"

"Because," answered Render, "he was a far nobler Roman than yourself."

"You lie! It is not so!"

Render shrugged and returned to the stabbing.

"It is not true!" screamed Caesar. "Not true!"

Render turned to him again and waved the dagger. Puppetlike, Caesar mimicked the pendulum of the blade.

"Not true?" Render smiled. "And who are you to question an assassination such as this? You are no one! You detract from the dignity of this occasion! Begone!"

Jerkily, the pink-faced man rose to his feet, his hair half-wispy, half-wetplastered, a disarray of cotton. He turned, moved away; and as he walked, he looked back over his shoulder.

He had moved far from the circle of assassins, but the scene did not diminish in size. It retained an electric clarity. It made him feel even further removed, ever more alone and apart.

Render rounded a previously unnoticed corner and stood before him, a blind beggar.

Caesar grasped the front of his garment.

"Have you an ill omen for me this day?"

"Beware!" jeered Render.

"Yes! Yes!" cried Caesar. " 'Beware!' That is good! Beware what?"

"The ides—"

"Yes? The ides—?"

"—of October."

He released the garment.

"What is that you say? What is Octember?"

"A month."

"You lie! There is no month of Octember!"

"And that is the date noble Caesar need fear—the non-existent time, the never-to-be-calendared occasion."

Render vanished around another sudden corner.

"Wait! Come back!"

Render laughed, and the Forum laughed with him. The bird-cries became a chorus of inhuman jeers.

"You mock me!" wept Caesar.

The Forum was an oven, and the perspiration formed like a glassy mask over Caesar's narrow forehead, sharp nose, chinless jaw.

"I want to be assassinated too!" he sobbed. "It isn't fair!"

And Render tore the Forum and the senators and the grinning corpse of Anthony to pieces and stuffed them into a black sack—with the unseen movement of a single finger—and last of all went Caesar.

Charles Render sat before the ninety white buttons and the two red ones, not really looking at any of them. His right arm moved in its soundless sling, across the lap-level surface of the console—pushing some of the buttons, skipping over others, moving on, retracing its path to press the next in the order of the Recall Series.

Sensations throttled, emotions reduced to nothing. Representative Erikson knew the oblivion of the womb.

There was a soft click.

Render's hand had glided to the end of the bottom row of buttons. An act of conscious intent—will, if you like —was required to push the red button.

Render freed his arm and lifted off his crown of Medusa-hair leads and microminiature circuitry. He slid from behind his desk-couch and raised the hood. He walked to the window and transpared it, fingering forth a cigarette.

One minute in the ro-womb, he decided. *No more. This is a crucial one . . . Hope it doesn't snow till later —these clouds look mean . . .*

It was smooth yellow trellises and high towers, glassy and gray, all smoldering into evening under a shale-colored sky; the city was squared volcanic islands, glowing in the end-of-day light, rumbling deep down under the earth; it was fat, incessant rivers of traffic, rushing.

Render turned away from the window and approached the great egg that lay beside his desk, smooth and glittering. It threw back a reflection that smashed all aquilinity from his nose, turned his eyes to gray saucers, transformed his hair into a light-streaked skyline; his reddish necktie became the wide tongue of a ghoul.

He smiled, reached across the desk. He pressed the second red button.

With a sigh, the egg lost its dazzling opacity and a horizontal crack appeared about its middle. Through the now-transparent shell, Render could see Erikson grimacing, squeezing his eyes tight, fighting against a return to consciousness and the thing it would contain. The upper half of the egg rose vertical to the base, exposing him knobby and pink on half-shell. When his eyes opened he did not look at Render. He rose to his feet and began dressing. Render used this time to check the ro-womb.

He leaned back across his desk and pressed the buttons: temperature control, full range, *check;* exotic sounds —he raised the earphone—*check,* on bells, on buzzes, on violin notes and whistles, on squeals and moans, on traffic noises and the sound of surf; *check,* on the feedback circuit—holding the patient's own voice, trapped earlier in analysis; *check,* on the sound blanket, the moisture spray, the odor banks; *check,* on the couch agitator and the colored lights, the taste stimulants. . . .

Render closed the egg and shut off its power. He pushed the unit into the closet, palmed shut the door. The tapes had registered a valid sequence.

"Sit down," he directed Erikson.

The man did so, fidgeting with his collar.

"You have full recall," said Render, "so there is no need for me to summarize what occurred. Nothing can be hidden from me. I was there."

Erikson nodded.

"The significance of the episode should be apparent to you."

Erikson nodded again, finally finding his voice. "But was it valid?" he asked. "I mean, you constructed the dream and you controlled it, all the way. I didn't really *dream* it—in the way I would normally dream. Your ability to make things happen stacks the deck for whatever you're going to say—doesn't it?"

Render shook his head slowly, flicked an ash into the southern hemisphere of his globe-made-ashtray, and met Erikson's eyes.

"It is true that I supplied the format and modified the forms. You, however, filled them with an emotional significance, promoted them to the status of symbols corresponding to your problem. If the dream was not a valid analogue it would not have provoked the reactions it did.

It would have been devoid of the anxiety-patterns which were registered on the tapes.

"You have been in analysis for many months now," he continued, "and everything I have learned thus far serves to convince me that your fears of assassination are without any basis in fact."

Erikson glared.

"Then why the hell do I have them?"

"Because," said Render, "you would like very much to be the subject of an assassination."

Erikson smiled then, his composure beginning to return.

"I assure you, doctor, I have never contemplated suicide, nor have I any desire to stop living."

He produced a cigar and applied a flame to it. His hand shook.

"When you came to me this summer," said Render, "you stated that you were in fear of an attempt on your life. You were quite vague as to why anyone should want to kill you—"

"My position! You can't be a Representative as long as I have and make no enemies!"

"Yet," replied Render, "it appears that you have managed it. When you permitted me to discuss this with your detectives I was informed that they could unearth nothing to indicate that your fears might have any real foundation. Nothing."

"They haven't looked far enough—or in the right places. They'll turn up something."

"I'm afraid not."

"Why?"

"Because, I repeat, your feelings are without any objective basis. Be honest with me. Have you any information whatsoever indicating that someone hates you enough to want to kill you?"

"I receive many threatening letters . . ."

"As do all Representatives—and all of those directed to you during the past year have been investigated and found to be the work of cranks. Can you offer me *one* piece of evidence to substantiate your claims?"

Erikson studied the tip of his cigar.

"I came to you on the advice of a colleague," he said, "came to you to have you poke around inside my mind to find me something of that sort, to give my detectives something to work with. Someone I've injured severely perhaps—or some damaging piece of legislation I've dealt with . . ."

"—And I found nothing," said Render, "nothing, that is, but the cause of your discontent. Now, of course, you are afraid to hear it, and you are attempting to divert me from explaining my diagnosis—"

"I am not!"

"Then, listen. You can comment afterwards if you want, but you've poked and dawdled around here for months, unwilling to accept what I presented to you in a dozen different forms. Now I am going to tell you outright what it is, and you can do what you want about it."

"Fine."

"First," he said, "you would like very much to have an enemy or enemies—"

"Ridiculous!"

"—Because it is the only alternative to having friends—"

"I have lots of friends!"

"—Because nobody wants to be completely ignored, to be an object for whom no one has really strong feelings.

11

Hatred and love are the ultimate forms of human regard. Lacking one, and unable to achieve it, you sought the other. You wanted it so badly that you succeeded in convincing yourself it existed. But there is always a psychic pricetag on these things. Answering a genuine emotional need with a body of desire-surrogates does not produce real satisfaction, but anxiety, discomfort—because in these matters the psyche should be an open system. You did not seek outside yourself for human regard. You were closed off. You created that which you needed from the stuff of your own being. You are a man very much in need of strong relationships with other people."

"Manure!"

"Take it or leave it," said Render. "I suggest you take it."

"I've been paying you for half a year to help find out who wants to kill me. Now you sit there and tell me I made the whole thing up to satisfy a desire to have someone hate me."

"Hate you, or love you. That's right."

"It's absurd! I meet so many people that I carry a pocket recorder and lapel-camera just so I can recall them all . . ."

"Meeting quantities of people is hardly what I was speaking of. Tell me, *did* that dream sequence have a strong meaning for you?"

Erikson was silent for several tickings of the huge wall-clock.

"Yes," he finally conceded, "it did. But your interpretation of the matter is still absurd. Granting, though, just for the sake of argument, that what is you say is correct—what would I do to get out of this bind?"

Render leaned back in his chair.

"Rechannel the energies that went into producing the

thing. Meet some people as yourself, Joe Erikson, rather than Representative Erikson. Take up something you can do with other people—something non-political, and perhaps somewhat competitive—and make some real friends or enemies, preferably the former. I've encouraged you to do this all along."

"Then tell me something else."

"Gladly."

"Assuming you *are* right, why is it that I am neither liked nor hated, and never have been? I have a responsible position in the Legislature. I meet people all the time. Why am I so neutral a—thing?"

Highly familiar now with Erikson's career, Render had to put aside his true thoughts on the matter, as they were of no operational value. He wanted to cite him Dante's observations concerning the trimmers—those souls who, denied heaven for their lack of virtue, were also denied entrance to hell for a lack of significant vices—in short, the ones who trimmed their sails to move them with every wind of the times, who lacked direction, who were not really concerned toward which ports they were pushed. Such was Erikson's long and colorless career of migrant loyalties, of political reversals.

Render said: "More and more people find themselves in such circumstances these days. It is due largely to the increasing complexity of society and the depersonalization of the individual into a sociometric unit. Even the act of cathecting toward other persons has grown more forced as a result. There are so many of us these days."

Erikson nodded, and Render smiled inwardly.

Sometimes the gruff line, and then the lecture . . .

"I've got the feeling you could be right," said Erikson. "Sometimes I *do* feel like what you just described—a unit, something depersonalized . . ."

Render glanced at the clock.

"What you choose to do about it from here is, of course, your own decision to make. I think you'd be wasting your time to remain in analysis any longer. We are now both aware of the cause of your complaint. I can't take you by the hand and show you how to lead your life. I can indicate, I can commiserate—but no more deep probing. Make an appointment as soon as you feel a need to discuss your activities and relate them to my diagnosis."

"I will"—Erickson nodded—"and damn that dream! It got to me. You can make them seem as vivid as waking life—more vivid . . . It may be a long while before I can forget it."

"I hope so."

"Okay, doctor." He rose to his feet, extended a hand. "I'll probably be back in a couple weeks. I'll give this socializing a fair try." He grinned at the word he normally frowned upon. "In fact, I'll start now. May I buy you a drink around the corner, downstairs?"

Render met the moist palm which seemed as weary of the performance as a lead actor in too successful a play. He felt almost sorry as he said, "Thank you, but I have an engagement."

Render helped him on with his coat then, handed him his hat, saw him to the door.

"Well, good night."

"Good night."

As the door closed soundlessly behind him, Render recrossed the dark Astrakhan to his mahogany fortress and flipped his cigarette into the southern hemisphere. He leaned back in his chair, hands behind his head, eyes closed.

"Of course it was more real than life," he informed no one in particular; "I shaped it."

Smiling, he reviewed the dream sequence step by step, wishing some of his former instructors could have witnessed it. It had been well-constructed and powerfully executed, as well as being precisely appropriate for the case at hand. But then, he was Render, the Shaper—one of the two hundred or so special analysts whose own psychic makeup permitted them to enter into neurotic patterns without carrying away more than an esthetic gratification from the mimesis of aberrance—a Sane Hatter.

Render stirred his recollections. He had been analyzed himself, analyzed and passed upon as a granite-willed, ultra-stable outsider—tough to weather the basilisk gaze of a fixation, walk unscathed amidst the chimarae of perversions, force dark Mother Medusa to close her eyes before the caduceus of his art. His own analysis had not been difficult. Nine years before (it seemed much longer) he had suffered a willing injection of novacain into the most painful area of his spirit. It was after the auto wreck, after the death of Ruth and of Miranda, their daughter, that he had begun to feel detached. Perhaps he did not want to recover certain empathies; perhaps his own world was now based upon a certain rigidity of feeling. If this was true, he was wise enough in the ways of the mind to realize it, and perhaps he had decided that such a world had its own compensations.

His son Peter was now ten years old. He was attending a school of quality, and he penned his father a letter every week. The letters were becoming progressively literate, showing signs of a precociousness of which Render could not but approve. He would take the boy with him to Europe in the summer.

As for Jill—Jill DeVille (what a luscious, ridiculous name!—he loved her for it)—she was growing, if anything, more interesting to him. (He wondered if this was an indication of early middle age.) He was vastly taken by her unmusical nasal voice, her sudden interest in architecture, her concern with the unremovable mole on the right side of her otherwise well-designed nose. He should really call her immediately and go in search of a new restaurant. For some reason, though, he did not feel like it.

It had been several weeks since he had visited his club, *The Partridge and Scalpel*, and he felt a strong desire to eat from an oaken table, alone, in the split-level dining room with the three fireplaces, beneath the artificial torches and the boars' heads like gin ads. So he pushed his perforated membership card into the phone-slot on his desk and there were two buzzes behind the voice-screen.

"Hello, *Partridge and Scalpel*," said the voice. "May I help you?"

"Charles Render," he said. "I'd like a table in about half an hour."

"How many will there be?"

"Just me."

"Very good, sir. Half an hour, then. That's 'Render'?—*R*-e-n-d-e-r?"

"Right."

"Thank you."

He broke the connection, rose from his desk. Outside, the day had vanished.

The monoliths and the towers gave forth their own light now. A soft snow, like sugar, was sifting down through the shadows and transforming itself into beads on the windowpane.

Render shrugged into his overcoat, turned off the lights, locked the inner office. There was a note on Mrs. Hedge's blotter.

Miss DeVille called, it said.

He crumpled the note and tossed it into the waste chute. He would call her tomorrow and say he had been working until late on his lecture.

He switched off the final light, clapped his hat onto his head and passed through the outer door, locking it as he went. The drop took him to the sub-subcellar where his auto was parked.

It was chilly in the sub-sub, and his footsteps seemed loud on the concrete as he passed among the parked vehicles. Beneath the glare of the naked lights, his S-7 Spinner was a sleek gray cocoon from which it seemed turbulent wings might at any moment emerge. The double row of antennae which fanned forward from the slope of its hood added to this feeling. Render thumbed open the door.

He touched the ignition and there was the sound of a lone bee awakening in a great hive. The door swung soundlessly shut as he raised the steering wheel and locked it into place. He spun up the spiral ramp and came to a rolling stop before the big overhead.

As the door rattled upward he lighted his destination screen and turned the knob that shifted the broadcast map. Left to right, top to bottom, section by section he shifted it, until he located the portion of Carnegi Avenue he desired. He punched out its coordinates and lowered the wheel. The car switched over to monitor and moved out onto the highway marginal. Render lit a cigarette.

Pushing his seat back into the centerspace, he left all the windows transparent. It was pleasant to half-recline and watch the oncoming cars drift past him like swarms of fireflies. He pushed his hat back on his head and stared upward.

He could remember a time when he had loved snow, when it had reminded him of novels by Thomas Mann and music by Scandinavian composers. In his mind now, though, there was another element from which it could never be wholly dissociated. He could visualize so clearly the eddies of milk-white coldness that swirled about his old manual-steer auto, flowing into its fire-charred interior to rewhiten that which had been blackened; so clearly— as though he had walked toward it across a chalky lake-bottom—it, the sunken wreck, and he, the diver—unable to open his mouth to speak, for fear of drowning; and he knew, whenever he looked upon falling snow, that somewhere skulls were whitening. But nine years had washed away much of the pain, and he also knew that the night was lovely.

He was sped along the wide, wide roads, shot across high bridges, their surfaces slick and gleaming beneath his lights, was woven through frantic clover leafs and plunged into a tunnel whose dimly glowing walls blurred by him like a mirage. Finally, he switched the windows to opaque and closed his eyes.

He could not remember whether he had dozed for a moment or not, which meant he probably had. He felt the car slowing, and he moved the seat forward and turned on the windows again. Almost simultaneously, the cut-off buzzer sounded. He raised the steering wheel and pulled into the parking dome, stepped out onto the ramp and left the car to the parking unit, receiving his ticket from that box-headed robot which took its solemn revenge on mankind by sticking forth a cardboard tongue at everyone it served.

As always, the noises were as subdued as the lighting. The place seemed to absorb sound and convert it into warmth, to lull the tongue with aromas strong enough to be tasted, to hypnotize the ear with the vivid crackle of the triple hearths.

Render was pleased to see that his favorite table, in the corner off to the right of the smaller fireplace, had been held for him. He knew the menu from memory, but he studied it with zeal as he sipped a Manhattan and worked up an order to match his appetite. Shaping sessions always left him ravenously hungry.

"Dr. Render . . . ?"

"Yes?" He looked up.

"Dr. Shallot would like to speak with you," said the waiter.

"I don't know anyone named Shallot," he said. "Are you sure he doesn't want Bender? He's a surgeon from Metro who sometimes eats here . . ."

The waiter shook his head.

"No sir—'Render.' See here?" He extended a three-by-five card on which Render's full name was typed in capital letters. "Dr. Shallot has dined here for nearly every night for the past two weeks," he explained, "and on each occasion has asked to be notified if you came in."

"Hm?" mused Render. "That's odd. Why didn't he just call me at my office?"

The waiter smiled and made a vague gesture.

"Well, tell him to come on over," he said, gulping his Manhattan, "and bring me another of these."

"Unfortunately, Dr. Shallot is blind," explained the waiter. "It would be easier if you—"

"All right, sure." Render stood up, relinquishing his favorite table with a strong premonition that he would not be returning to it that evening.

"Lead on."

They threaded their way among the diners, heading up to the next level. A familiar face said "hello" from a table set back against the wall, and Render nodded a greeting to a former seminar pupil whose name was Jurgens or Jirkans or something like that.

He moved on, into the smaller dining room wherein only two tables were occupied. No, three. There was one set in the corner at the far end of the darkened bar, partly masked by an ancient suit of armor. The waiter was heading him in that direction.

They stopped before the table and Render stared down into the darkened glasses that had tilted upward as they approached. Dr. Shallot was a woman, somewhere in the vicinity of her early thirties. Her low bronze bangs did not fully conceal the spot of silver which she wore on her forehead like a caste-mark. Render inhaled, and her head jerked slightly as the tip of his cigarette flared. She appeared to be staring straight up into his eyes. It was an uncomfortable feeling, even knowing that all she could distinguish of him was that which her minute photoelectric cell transmitted to her visual cortex over the hair-fine wire implants attached to that oscillator-converter: in short, the glow of his cigarette.

"Dr. Shallot, this is Dr. Render," the waiter was saying.

"Good evening," said Render.

"Good evening," she said. "My name is Eileen and I've wanted very badly to meet you." He thought he detected a slight quaver in her voice. "Will you join me for dinner?"

"My pleasure," he acknowledged, and the waiter drew out the chair.

Render sat down, noting that the woman across from

him already had a drink. He reminded the waiter of his second Manhattan.

"Have you ordered yet?" he inquired.

"No."

". . . And two menus—" he started to say, then bit his tongue.

"Only one." She smiled.

"Make it none," he amended, and recited the menu.

They ordered. Then:

"Do you always do that?"

"What?"

"Carry menus in your head."

"Only a few," he said, "for awkward occasions. What was it you wanted to see—talk to me about?"

"You're a neuroparticipant therapist," she stated, "a Shaper."

"And you are—?"

"—a resident in psychiatry at State Psych. I have a year remaining."

"You knew Sam Riscomb then."

"Yes, he helped me get my appointment. He was my adviser."

"He was a very good friend of mine. We studied together at Menninger."

She nodded.

"I'd often heard him speak of you—that's one of the reasons I wanted to meet you. He's responsible for encouraging me to go ahead with my plans, despite my handicap."

Render stared at her. She was wearing a dark green dress which appeared to be made of velvet. About three inches to the left of the bodice was a pin which might have been gold. It displayed a red stone which could have been a ruby, around which the outline of a goblet was cast. Or was it really two profiles that were outlines, staring through the stone at one another? It seemed vaguely familiar to him, but he could not place it at the moment. It glittered expensively in the dim light.

Render accepted his drink from the waiter.

"I want to become a neuroparticipant therapist," she told him.

And if she had possessed vision Render would have thought she was staring at him, hoping for some response in his expression. He could not quite calculate what she wanted him to say.

"I commend your choice," he said, "and I respect your ambition." He tried to put his smile into his voice. "It is not an easy thing, of course, not all of the requirements being academic ones."

"I know," she said. "But then, I have been blind since birth and it was not an easy thing to come this far."

"Since birth?" he repeated. "I thought you might have lost your sight recently. You did your undergrad work then, and went on through med school without eyes . . . That's—rather impressive."

"Thank you," she said, "but it isn't. Not really. I heard about the first neuroparticipants—Bartelmetz and the rest—when I was a child, and I decided then that I want to be one. My life ever since has been governed by that desire."

"What did you do in the labs?" he inquired. "—Not being able to see a specimen, look through a microscope . . . ? Or all that reading?"

"I hired people to read my assignments to me. I taped everything. The school understood that I wanted to go into psychiatry, and they permitted a special arrangement for labs. I've been guided through the dissection of cadavers by lab assistants, and I've had everything described to me. I can tell things by touch . . . and I have a memory like yours with the menu." She smiled. " 'The quality of psychoparticipation phenomena can only be gauged by the therapist himself, at that moment outside of time and space as we normally know it, when he stands in the midst of a world erected from the stuff of another man's dreams, recognizes there the non-Euclidian architecture of aberrance, and then takes his patient by the hand and tours the landscape . . . If he can lead him back to the common earth, then his judgments were sound, his actions valid.' "

"From *Why No Psychometrics in This Place*," reflected Render.

"—by Charles Render, M.D."

"Our dinner is already moving in this direction," he noted, picking up his drink as the speed-cooked meal was pushed toward them in the kitchen-buoy.

"That's one of the reasons I wanted to meet you," she continued, raising her glass as the dishes rattled before her. "I want you to help me become a Shaper."

Her shaded eyes, as vacant as a statue's, sought him again.

"Yours is a completely unique situation," he commented. "There has never been a congenitally blind neuro-participant—for obvious reasons. I'd have to consider all the aspects of the situation before I could advise you. Let's eat now, though. I'm starved."

"All right. But my blindness does not mean that I have never seen."

He did not ask her what she meant by that, because prime ribs were standing in front of him now and there was a bottle of Chambertin at his elbow. He did pause long enough to notice though, as she raised her left hand from beneath the table, that she wore no rings.

"I wonder if it's still snowing," he commented as they drank their coffee. "It was coming down pretty hard when I pulled into the dome."

"I hope so," she said, "even though it diffuses the light and I can't 'see' anything at all through it. I like to feel it falling about me and blowing against my face."

"How do you get about?"

"My dog, Sigmund—I gave him the night off," she smiled—"he can guide me anywhere. He's a mutie Shepherd."

"Oh?" Render grew curious. "Can he talk much?"

She nodded.

"That operation wasn't as successful on him as on some of them, though. He has a vocabulary of about four hundred words, but I think it causes him pain to speak. He's quite intelligent. You'll have to meet him sometime."

Render began speculating immediately. He had spoken with such animals at recent medical conferences, and had been startled by their combination of reasoning ability and their devotion to their handlers. Much chromosome tinkering, followed by delicate embryo-surgery, was required to give a dog a brain capacity greater than a chimpanzee's. Several followup operations were necessary to produce vocal abilities. Most such experiments ended in failure, and the dozen or so puppies a year on which they succeeded were valued in the neighborhood of a hundred thousand dollars each. He realized then, as he lit a cigarette and held the light for a moment, that the stone in Miss Shallot's medallion was a genuine ruby. He began to suspect that her admission to a medical school might, in addition to her academic record, have been based upon a sizable endowment to the college of her choice. Perhaps he was being unfair though, he chided himself.

"Yes," he said, "we might do a paper on canine neuroses. Does he ever refer to his father as 'that son of a female Shepherd'?"

"He never met his father," she said, quite soberly. "He was raised apart from other dogs. His attitude could hardly be typical. I don't think you'll ever learn the functional psychology of the dog from a mutie."

"I imagine you're right," he dismissed it. "More coffee?"

"No, thanks."

Deciding it was time to continue the discussion, he said, "So you want to be a Shaper . . ."

"Yes."

"I hate to be the one to destroy anybody's high ambitions," he told her. "Like poison, I hate it. Unless they have no foundation at all in reality. Then I can be ruthless. So—honestly, frankly, and in all sincerity, I do not see how it could ever be managed. Perhaps you're a fine psychiatrist—but in my opinion, it is a physical and mental impossibility for you ever to become a neuroparticipant. As for my reasons—"

"Wait," she said. "Not here, please. Humor me. I'm tired of this stuffy place—take me somewhere else to talk. I think I might be able to convince you there *is* a way."

"Why not?" He shrugged. "I have plenty time. Sure—you call it. Where?"

"Blindspin?"

He suppressed an unwilling chuckle at the expression, but she laughed aloud.

"Fine," he said, "but I'm still thirsty."

A bottle of champagne was tallied and he signed the check despite her protests. It arrived in a colorful "Drink While You Drive" basket, and they stood then, and she was tall, but he was taller.

Blindspin.

A single name of a multitude of practices centered about the auto-driven auto. Flashing across the country in the sure hands of an invisible chauffeur, windows all opaque, night dark, sky high, tires assailing the road below like four phantom buzzsaws—and starting from scratch and ending in the same place, and never knowing where you are going or where you have been—it is possible, for a moment, to kindle some feeling of individuality in the coldest brainpan, to produce a momentary awareness of self by virtue of an apartness from all but a sense of motion. This is because movement through darkness is the ultimate abstraction of life itself—at least that's what one of the Vital Comedians said, and everybody in the place laughed.

Actually now, the phenomenon known as blindspin first became prevalent (as might be suspected) among certain younger members of the community, when monitored highways deprived them of the means to exercise their automobiles in some of the more individualistic ways which had come to be frowned upon by the National Traffic Control Authority. Something had to be done.

It was.

The first, disastrous reaction involved the simple engineering feat of disconnecting the broadcast control unit after one had entered onto a monitored highway. This resulted in the car's vanishing from the ken of the monitor and passing back into the control of its occupants. Jealous as a deity, a monitor will not tolerate that which denies its programmed omniscience; it will thunder and lightning in the Highway Control Station nearest the point of last contact, sending winged seraphs in search of was, at first, relatively easy to achieve.

Often, however, this was too late in happening, for the roads are many and well-paved. Escape from detection was, at first, reltively esy to afhieve.

Other vehicles, though, necessarily behave as if a rebel has no actual existence. Its presence cannot be allowed for.

Boxed-in, on a heavily-traveled section of roadway, the offender is subject to immediate annihilation in the event of any overall speedup or shift in traffic pattern which involves movement through his theoretically vacant position. This, in the early days of monitor controls, caused a rapid series of collisions. Monitoring devices later became far more sophisticated, and mechanized cutoffs reduced the collision incidence subsequent to such an action. The quality of the pulpefactions and contusions which did occur, however remained unaltered.

The next reaction was based on a thing which had been overlooked because it was obvious. The monitors took people where they wanted to go only because people told them they wanted to go there. A person pressing a random series of coordinates, without reference to any map, would either be left with a stalled automobile and a "RECHECK YOUR COORDINATES" light, or would suddenly be whisked away in any direction. The latter possesses a certain romantic appeal in that it offers speed, unexpected sights, and free hands. Also, it is perfectly legal; and it is possible to navigate all over two continents in this manner, if one is possessed of sufficient wherewithal and gluteal stamina.

As in the case in all such matters, the practice diffused upwards through the age brackets. School teachers who only drove on Sundays fell into disrepute as selling points for used autos. Such is the way a world ends, said the entertainer.

End or no, the car designed to move on monitored highways is a mobile efficiency unit, complete with latrine, cupboard, refrigerator compartment and gaming table. It also sleeps two with ease and four with some crowding. On occasion, three can be a real crowd.

Render drove out of the dome and into the marginal aisle. He halted the car.

"Want to jab some coordinates?" he asked.

"You do it. My fingers know too many."

Render punched random buttons. The Spinner moved onto the highway. Render asked speed of the vehicle then, and it moved into the high-acceleration lane.

The Spinner's lights burnt holes in the darkness. The city backed away fast; it was a smoldering bonfire on both sides of the road, stirred by sudden gusts of wind, hidden by white swirlings, obscured by the steady fall of gray ash. Render knew his speed was only about sixty percent of what it would have been on a clear, dry night.

He did not blank the windows, but leaned back and stared out through them. Eileen "looked" ahead into what light there was. Neither of them said anything for ten or fifteen minutes.

The city shrank to sub-city as they sped on. After a time, short sections of open road began to appear.

"Tell me what it looks like outside," she said.

"Why didn't you ask me to describe your dinner, or the suit of armor beside our table?"

"Because I tasted one and felt the other. This is different."

"There is snow falling outside. Take it away and what you have left is black."

"What else?"

"There is slush on the road. When it starts to freeze, traffic will drop to a crawl unless we outrun this storm. The slush looks like an old, dark syrup, just starting to get sugary on top."

"Anything else?"

"That's it, lady."

"Is it snowing harder or less hard than when we left the club?"

"Harder, I should say."

"Would you pour me a drink?" she asked him.

"Certainly."

They turned their seats inward and Render raised the table. He fetched two glasses from the cupboard.

"Your health," said Render, after he had poured.

"Here's looking at you."

Render downed his drink. She sipped hers. He waited for her next comment. He knew that two cannot play at the Socratic game, and he expected more questions before she said what she wanted to say.

She said: "What is the most beautiful thing you have ever seen?"

Yes, he decided, and he guessed correctly.

He replied with out hesitation: "The sinking of Atlantis."

"I was serious."

"So was I."

"Would you care to elaborate?"

"I sank Atlantis," he said, "personally.

"It was about three years ago. And God! it was lovely! It was all ivory towers and golden minarets and silver balconies. There were bridges of opal, and crimson pennants and a milk-white river flowing between lemon-colored banks. There were jade steeples, and trees as old as the world tickling the bellies of clouds, and ships in the great sea-harbor of Xanadu, as delicately constructed as musical instruments, all swaying with the tides. The twelve princes of the realm held court in the dozen-pillared Coliseum of the Zodiac, to listen to a Greek tenor sax play at sunset.

"The Greek, of course, was a patient of mine—paranoiac. The etiology of the thing is rather complicated, but that's what I wandered into inside his mind. I gave him free rein for awhile, and in the end I had to split Atlantis in half and sink it full fathom five. He's playing again and you've doubtless heard his sounds, if you like such sounds at all. He's good. I still see him periodically, but he is no longer the last descendant of the greatest minstrel of Atlantis. He's just a fine, late twentieth-century sax-man.

"Sometimes though, as I look back on the apocalypse I worked within his vision of grandeur, I experience a fleeting sense of lost beauty—because, for a single moment, his abnormally intense feelings were my feelings, and he felt that his dream was the most beautiful thing in the world."

He refilled their glasses.

"That wasn't exactly what I meant," she said.

"I know."

"I meant something real."

"It was more real than real, I assure you."

"I don't doubt it, but . . ."

"—But I destroyed the foundation you were laying for your argument. Okay, I apologize. I'll hand it back to you. Here's something that could be real:

"We are moving along the edge of a great bowl of sand," he said. "Into it, the snow is gently drifting. In the spring the snow will melt, the waters will run down into the earth, or be evaporated away by the heat of the sun. Then only the sand will remain. Nothing grows in the sand, except for an occasional cactus. Nothing lives here but snakes, a few birds, insects, burrowing things, and a wandering coyote or two. In the afternoon these things will look for shade. Any place where there's an old fence post or a rock or a skull or a cactus to block out the sun, there you will witness life cowering before the elements. But the colors are beyond belief, and the elements are more lovely, almost, than the things they destroy."

"There is no such place near here," she said.

"If I say it, then there is. Isn't there? I've seen it."

"Yes . . . You're right."

"And it doesn't matter if it's a painting by a woman named O'Keefe, or something right outside our window, does it? If I've seen it?"

"I acknowledge the truth of the diagnosis," she said. "Do you want to speak it for me?"

"No, go ahead."

He refilled the small glasses once more.

"The damage is in my eyes," she told him, "not my brain."

He lit her cigarette.

"I can see with other eyes if I can enter other brains."

He lit his own cigarette.

31

"Neuroparticipation is based upon the fact that two nervous systems can share the same impulses, the same fantasies . . ."

"*Controlled* fantasies."

"I could perform therapy and at the same time experience genuine visual impressions."

"No," said Render.

"You don't know what it's like to be cut off from a whole area of stimuli! To know that a Mongoloid idiot can experience something you can never know—and that he cannot appreciate it because, like you, he was condemned before birth in a court of biological hapstance, in a place where there is no justice—only fortuity, pure and simple."

"The universe did not invent justice. Man did. Unfortunately, man must reside in the universe."

"I'm not asking the universe to help me—I'm asking you."

"I'm sorry," said Render.

"Why won't you help me?"

"At this moment you are demonstrating my main reason."

"Which is . . . ?"

"Emotion. This thing means far too much to you. When the therapist is in-phase with a patient he is narcoelectrically removed from most of his own bodily sensations. This is necessary—because his mind must be completely absorbed by the task at hand. It is also necessary that his emotions undergo a similar suspension. This, of course, is impossible in the one sense that a person always emotes to some degree. But the therapist's emotions are sublimated into a generalized feeling of exhilaration—or, as in my own case, into an artistic reverie. With you, however, the 'seeing' would be too much. You would be in constant danger of losing control of the dream."

"I disagree with you."

"Of course you do. But the fact remains that you would be dealing, and dealing constantly, with the abnormal. The power of a neurosis is unimaginable to ninety-nine point etcetera percent of the population, because we can never adequately judge the intensity of our own— let alone those of others, when we only see them from the outside. That is why no neuroparticipant will ever undertake to treat a full-blown psychotic. The few pioneers in that area are all themselves in therapy today. It would be like driving into a maelstrom. If the therapist loses the upper hand in an intense session he becomes the Shaped rather than the Shaper. The synopses respond like a fission reaction when nervous impulses are artificially augmented. The transference effect is almost instantaneous.

"I did an awful lot of skiing five years ago. This is because I was a claustrophobe. I had to run and it took me six months to beat the thing—all because of one tiny lapse that occurred in a measureless fraction of an instant. I had to refer the patient to another therapist. And this was only a minor repercussion. If you were to go ga-ga over the scenery, girl, you could wind up in a rest home for life."

She finished her drink and Render refilled the glass. The night raced by. They had left the city far behind them, and the road was open and clear. The darkness eased more and more of itself between the falling flakes. The Spinner picked up speed.

"All right," she admitted, "maybe you're right. Still, though, I think you can help me."

"How?" he asked.

"Accustom me to seeing, so that the images will lose their novelty, the emotions wear off. Accept me as a patient and rid me of my sight-anxiety. Then what you have said so far will cease to apply. I will be able to undertake the training then, and give my full attention to therapy. I'll be able to sublimate the sight-pleasure into something else."

Render wondered.

Perhaps it could be done. It would be a difficult undertaking, though.

It might also make therapeutic history.

No one was really qualified to try it, because no one had ever tried it before.

But Eileen Shallot was a rarity—no, a unique item—for it was likely she was the only person in the world who combined the necessary technical background with the unique problem.

He drained his glass, refilled it, refilled hers.

He was still considering the problem as the "RE-CO-ORDINATE" light came on and the car pulled into a cutoff and stood there. He switched off the buzzer and sat there for a long while, thinking.

It was not often that other persons heard him acknowledge his feelings regarding his skill. His colleagues considered him modest. Offhand, though, it might be noted that he was aware that the day a better neuroparticipant began practicing would be the day that a troubled Homo sapien was to be treated by something but immeasurably less than angels.

Two drinks remained. Then he tossed the emptied bottle into the backbin.

"You know something?" he finally said.

"What?"

"It might be worth a try."

He swiveled about then and leaned forward to re-co-ordinate, but she was there first. As he pressed the buttons and the S-7 swung around, she kissed him. Below her dark glasses her cheeks were moist.

II

THE SUICIDE bothered him more than it should have, and Mrs. Lambert had called the day before to cancel her appointment. So Render decided to spend the morning being pensive. Accordingly, he entered the office wearing a cigar and a frown.

"Did you see . . . ?" asked Mrs. Hedges.

"Yes." He pitched his coat onto the table that stood in the far corner of the room. He crossed to the window, stared down. "Yes," he repeated, "I was driving by with my windows clear. They were still cleaning up when I passed."

"Did you know him?"

"I don't even know the name yet. How could I?"

"Priss Tully just called me—she's a receptionist for that engineering outfit up on the eighty-sixth. She says it was James Irizarry, an ad designer who had offices down the hall from them. That's a long way to fall. He must have been unconscious when he hit, huh? He bounced off the building. If you open the window and lean out you can see—off to the left there—where . . ."

"Never mind, Bennie. Your friend have any idea why he did it?"

"Not really. His secretary came running up the hall, screaming. Seems she went in his office to see him about

36

some drawings, just as he was getting over the sill. There was a note on his board. 'I've had everything I wanted.' it said. 'Why wait around?' Sort of funny, huh? I don't mean *funny* . . ."

"Yeah . . . Know anything about his personal affairs?"

"Married. Coupla kids. Good professional rep. Lots of business. Sober as anybody. He could afford an office in this building."

"Good Lord!" Render turned. "Have you got a case file there or something?"

"You know," she shrugged her thick shoulders, "I've got friends all over this hive. We always talk when things go slow. Prissy's my sister-in-law anyhow—"

"You mean that if I dived through this window right now, my current biography would make the rounds in the next five minutes?"

"Probably"—she twisted her bright lips into a smile—"give or take a couple. But don't do it today, huh? You know, it would be kind of anticlimactic, and it wouldn't get the same coverage as a solus.

"Anyhow," she continued, "you're a mind-mixer. You wouldn't do it."

"You're betting against statistics," he observed. "The medical profession, along with attorneys, manages about three times as many as most other work areas."

"Hey!" she looked worried. "Go 'way from my window!

"I'd have to go to work for Dr. Hanson then," she added, "and he's a slob."

He moved to her desk.

"I never know when to take you seriously," she decided.

"I appreciate your concern"—he nodded—"indeed I do. As a matter of fact, I have never been statistic-prone

—I should have repercussed out of the neuropy game four years ago."

"You'd be a headline, though," she mused. "All those reporters asking me about you . . . Hey, why do they do it, huh?"

"Who?"

"Anybody."

"How should I know, Bennie? I'm only a humble psyche-stirrer. If I could pinpoint a general underlying cause—and then maybe figure a way to anticipate the thing—why, it might even be better than my jumping, for newscopy. But I can't do it, because there is no single, simple reason—I don't think."

"Oh."

"About thirty-five years ago it was the ninth leading cause of death in the United States. Now it's number six for North and South America. I think it's seventh in Europe."

"And nobody will ever really know why Irizarry jumped?"

Render swung a chair backwards and seated himself. He knocked an ash into her petite and gleaming tray. She emptied it into the waste-chute, hastily, and coughed a significant cough.

"Oh, one can always speculate," he said, "and one in my profession will. The first thing to consider would be the personality traits which might predispose a man to periods of depression. People who keep their emotions under rigid control, people who are conscientious and rather compulsively concerned with small matters . . ." He knocked another fleck of ash into her tray and watched as she reached out to dump, then quickly drew her hand back again. He grinned an evil grin. "In short," he finished, "some of the characteristics of people in professions which require individual, rather than group performance—medicine, law, the arts."

She regarded him speculatively.

"Don't worry though—" he chuckled—"I'm pleased as hell with life."

"You're kind of down in the mouth this morning."

"Peter called me. He broke his ankle yesterday in gym class. They ought to supervise those things more closely. I'm thinking of changing his school."

"Again?"

"Maybe. I'll see. The headmaster is going to call me this afternoon. I don't like to keep shuffling him, but I do want him to finish school in one piece."

"A kid can't grow up without an accident or two. It's—statistics."

"Statistics aren't the same thing as destiny, Bennie. Everybody makes his own."

"Statistics or destiny?"

"Both, I guess."

"I think that if something's going to happen, it's going to happen."

"I don't. I happen to think that the human will, backed by a sane mind can exercise some measure of control over events. If I didn't think so, I wouldn't be in the racket I'm in."

"The world's a machine—you know—cause, effect. Statistics do imply the prob—"

"The human mind is not a machine, and I do not know cause and effect. Nobody does."

"You have a degree in chemistry, as I recall. You're a scientist, Doc."

"So I'm a Trotskyite deviationist"—he smiled, stretching—"and you were once a ballet teacher." He got to his feet and picked up his coat.

"By the way, Miss Deville called, left a message. She said: 'How about St. Moritz?' "

"Too ritzy," he decided aloud. "It's going to be Davos."

Because the suicide bothered him more than it should have, Render closed the door of his office and turned off the windows and turned on the phonograph. He put on the desk light only.

How has the quality of human life been changed, he wrote, *since the beginnings of the industrial revolution?*

He picked up the paper and reread the sentence. It was the topic he had been asked to discuss that coming Saturday. As was typical in such cases he did not know what to say because he had too much to say, and only an hour to say it in.

He got up and began to pace the office, now filled with Beethoven's Eighth Symphony.

"The power to hurt," he said, snapping on a lapel microphone and activating his recorder, "has evolved in a direct relationship to technological advancement." His imaginary audience grew quiet. He smiled. "Man's potential for working simple mayhem has been multiplied by mass-production; his capacity for injuring the psyche through personal contacts has expanded in an exact ratio to improved communication facilities. But these are all matters of common knowledge, and are not the things I wish to consider tonight. Rather, I should like to discuss what I choose to call autopsy-chomimesis—the self-generated anxiety complexes which on first scrutiny appear quite similar to classic patterns, but which actually represent radical dispersions of psychic energy. They are peculiar to our times . . ."

He paused to dispose of his cigar and formulate his next words.

"Autopsychomimesis," he thought aloud, "a self-perpetuated imitation complex—almost an attention-getting affair. A jazzman, for example, who acted hopped-up half the time, even though he had never used an addictive narcotic and only dimly remembered anyone who had—because all the stimulants and tranquilizers of today are quite benign. Like Quixote, he aspired after a legend when his music alone should have been sufficient outlet for his tensions.

"Or my Korean War Orphan, alive today by virtue of the Red Cross and UNICEF and foster parents whom he never met. He wanted a family so badly that he made one up. And what then?—He hated his imaginary father and he loved his imaginary mother quite dearly—for he was a highly intelligent boy, and he too longed after the half-true complexes of tradition. Why?"

"Today, everyone is sophisticated enough to understand the time-honored patterns of psychic disturbance. Today, many of the reasons for those disturbances have been removed—not radically as my now-adult war orphan's, but with as remarkable an effect. We are living in a neurotic past. —Again, why? Because our present times are geared to physical health, security and well-being. We have abolished hunger, though the backwoods orphan would still rather receive a package of food concentrates from a human being who cares for him than to obtain a warm meal from an automat unit in the middle of the jungle.

"Physical welfare is now every man's right, in excess. The reaction to this has occurred in the area of mental health. Thanks to technology, the reasons for many of the old social problems have passed, and along with them went many of the reasons for psychic distress. But between the black of yesterday and the white of tomorrow is the great gray of today, filled with nostalgia and fear of the future, which cannot be expressed on a purely material plane, is now being represented by a willful seeking after historical anxiety-modes . . ."

The phone-box puzzed briefly. Render did not hear it over the Eighth.

"We are afraid of what we do not know," he continued, "and tomorrow is a very great unknown. My own specialized area of psychiatry did not even exist thirty years ago. Science is capable of advancing itself so rapidly now that there is a genuine public uneasiness —I might even say 'distress'—as to the logical outcome: the total mechanization of everything in the world. . . ."

He passed near the desk as the phone buzzed again. He switched off his microphone and softened the Eighth.

"Hello?"

"Saint Moritz?" she said.

"Davos," he replied firmly.

"Charlie, you are most exasperating!"

"Jill, dear—so are you."

"Shall we discuss it tonight?"

"There is nothing to discuss!"

"You'll pick me up at five, though?"

He hesitated, then;

"Yes, at five. How come the screen is blank?"

"I've had my hair fixed. I'm going to surprise you again."

He suppressed an idiot chuckle said, "Pleasantly, I hope. Okay, see you then," waited for her "good-bye," and broke the connection.

He transpared the windows, turned off the light on his desk, and looked outside.

Gray again overhead, and many slow flakes of snow— wandering, not being blown about much—moving downwards and then losing themselves in the tumult. . . .

He also saw, when he opened the window and leaned out, the place off to the left where Irizarry had left his next-to-last mark on the world.

He closed the window and listened to the rest of the symphony. It had been a week since he had gone blind-spinning with Eileen. Her appointment was for one o'clock.

He remembered her fingertips brushing over his face, like leaves or the bodies of insects, learning his appearance in the ancient manner of the blind. The memory was not altogether pleasant. He wondered why.

Far below, a patch of hosed pavement was blank once again; under a thin, fresh shroud of white, it was slippery as glass. A building custodian hurried outside and spread salt on it, before someone slipped and hurt himself.

Sigmund was the myth of the Fenris come alive. After Render had instructed Mrs. Hedges, "Show them in," the door had begun to open, was suddenly pushed wider, and a pair of smoky-yellow eyes stared in at him. The eyes were set in a strangely misshapen dog-skull.

Sigmund's was not a low canine brow, slanting up slightly from the muzzle; it was a high, shaggy cranium, making the eyes appear even more deep-set than they actually were. Render shivered slightly at the size and aspect of that head. The muties he had seen had all been puppies. Sigmund was full grown, and his gray-black fur had a tendency to bristle, which made him appear somewhat larger than a normal specimen of the breed.

He stared in at Render in a very un-doglike way and made a growling noise which sounded too much like, "Hello, Doctor," to have been an accident.

Render nodded and stood.

"Hello, Sigmund," he said. "Come in."

The dog turned his head, sniffing the air of the room—as though deciding whether or not to trust his ward within its confines. Then he returned his stare to Render, dipped his head in an affirmative, and shouldered the door open. Perhaps the entire encounter had taken only one disconcerting second.

Eileen followed him, holding lightly to the double-leashed harness. The dog padded soundlessly across the thick rug—head low, as though he was stalking something. His eyes never left Render's.

"So this is Sigmund . . . ? How are you, Eileen?"

"Fine . . . Yes, he wanted very badly to come along, and *I* wanted you to meet him."

Render led her to a chair and seated her. She unsnapped the double guide from the dog's harness and placed it on the floor. Sigmund sat down beside it and continued to stare at Render.

"How is everything at State Psych?"

"Same as always. May I bum a cigarette, Doctor? I forgot mine."

He placed it between her fingers, furnishing a light. She was wearing a dark blue suit and her glasses were flame blue. The silver spot on her forehead reflected the glow of his lighter; she continued to stare at that point in space after he had withdrawn his hand. Her shoulder-length hair appeared a trifle lighter than it had seemed on the night they met; today it was like a fresh-minted copper coin.

Render seated himself on the corner of his desk, drawing up his world-ashtray with his toe.

"You told me before that being blind did not mean that

you had never seen. I didn't ask you to explain it then. But I'd like to ask you now."

"I had a neuroparticipation session with Dr. Riscomb," she told him, "before he had his accident. He wanted to accommodate my mind to visual impressions. Unfortunately, there was never a second session."

"I see. What did you do in that session?"

She crossed her ankles and Render noted they were well-turned.

"Colors, mostly. The experience was quite overwhelming."

"How well do you remember them? How long ago was it?"

"About six months ago—and I shall never forget them. I have even dreamt in color patterns since then."

"How often?"

"Several times a week."

"What sort of associations do they carry?"

"Nothing special. They just come into my mind along with other stimuli now—in a pretty haphazard way."

"How?"

"Well, for instance, when you ask me a question it's a sort of yellowish-orangish pattern that I 'see.' Your greeting was a kind of silvery thing. Now that you're just sitting there listening to me, saying nothing, I associate you with a deep, almost violet, blue."

Sigmund shifted his gaze to the desk and stared at the side panel.

Can he hear the recorder spinning inside? wondered Render. *And if he can, can he guess what it is and what it's doing?*

If so, the dog would doubtless tell Eileen—not that she was unaware of what was now an accepted practice

—and she might not like being reminded that he considered her case as therapy, rather than a mere mechanical adaptation process. If he thought it would do any good (he smiled inwardly at the notion), he would talk to the dog in private about it.

Inwardly, he shrugged.

"I'll construct a rather elementary fantasy world then," he said finally, "and introduce you to some basic forms today."

She smiled; and Render looked down at the myth who crouched by her side, its tongue a piece of beefsteak hanging over a picket fence.

Is he smiling too?

"Thank you," she said.

Sigmund wagged his tail.

"Well then"—Render disposed of his cigarette near Madagascar—"I'll fetch out the 'egg' now and test it. In the meantime"—he pressed an unobtrusive button—"perhaps some music would prove relaxing."

She started to reply, but a Wagnerian overture snuffed out the words. Render jammed the button again, and there was a moment of silence during which he said, "Heh heh. Thought Respighi was next."

It took two more pushes for him to locate some Roman Pines.

"You could have left him on," she observed. "I'm quite fond of Wagner."

"No thanks," he said, opening the closet, "I'd keep stepping in all those piles of leitmotifs."

The great egg drifted out into the office, soundless as a cloud. Render heard a soft growl behind as he drew it toward the desk. He turned quickly.

Like the shadow of a bird, Sigmund had gotten to his feet, crossed the room, and was already circling the machine and sniffing at it—tail taut, ears flat, teeth bared.

"Easy, Sig," said Render. "It's an Omnichannel Neural T & R Unit. It won't bite or anything like that. It's just a machine, like a car, teevee, or dishwasher. That's what we're going to use today to show Eileen what some things look like."

"Don't like it," rumbled the dog.

"Why?"

Sigmund had no reply, so he stalked back to Eileen and laid his head in her lap.

"Dont like it," he repeated, looking up at her.

"Why?"

"No words," he decided. "We go home now?"

"No." she answered him. "You're going to curl up in the corner and take a nap, and I'm going to curl up in that machine and do the same thing—sort of."

"No good," he said, tail drooping.

"Go on now"—she pushed him—"lie down and behave yourself."

He acquiesced, but he whined when Render blanked the windows and touched the button which transformed his desk into the operator's seat.

He whined once more—when the egg, connected now to an outlet, broke in the middle and the top slid back and up, revealing the interior.

Render seated himself. His chair became a contour couch and moved in halfway beneath the console. He sat upright and it moved back again, becoming a chair. He touched a part of the desk and half the ceiling disengaged itself, reshaped itself, and lowered to hover overhead like a huge bell. He stood and moved around to the side of the ro-womb. Respighi spoke of pines and such, and Render disengaged an earphone from beneath the egg and leaned back beneath the egg and leaned across his desk. Blocking one ear with his shoulder and pressing the microphone to the other, he played upon the buttons with his free hand. Leagues of surf drowned the tone poem; miles of traffic overrode it and the feedback said: ". . . Now that you are just sitting there listening to me, saying nothing, I associate you with a deep, almost violet, blue . . ."

He switched to the face mask and monitored *one*— cinnamon, *two*—leaf mold, *three* deep reptilian musk . . . and down through thirst, and the tastes of honey and vinegar and salt, and back on up through lilacs and wet concrete, a before-the-storm whiff of ozone, and all the basic olfactory and gustatory cues for morning, afternoon and evening.

The couch floated normally in its pool of mercury, magnetically stabilized by the walls of the egg. He set the tapes.

The ro-womb was in perfect condition.

"Okay," said Render, turning, "everything checks."

She was just placing her glasses atop her folded garments. She had undressed while Render was testing the machine. He was perturbed by her narrow waist, her large, dark-pointed breasts, her long legs. She was too well-formed for a woman her height, he decided.

He realized though, as he stared at her, that his main annoyance was, of course, the fact that she was his patient.

"Ready here," she said, and he moved to her side.

He took her below and guided her to the machine. Her fingers explored its interior. As he helped her enter the unit, he saw that her eyes were a vivid sea-green. Of this, too, he disapproved.

"Comfortable?"

"Yes."

"Okay we're set. I'm going to close it. Sweet dreams."

The upper shell dropped slowly. Closed, it grew opaque, then dazzling. Render was staring down at his own distorted reflection.

He moved back in the direction of his desk.

Sigmund was on his feet, blocking the way.

Render reached down to pat his head, but the dog jerked it aside.

"Take me, with," he growled.

"I'm afraid that can't be done, old fellow," said Render. "Besides, we're not really going anywhere. We'll just be dozing, right here, in this room."

The dog did not seem mollified.

"Why?"

Render sighed. An argument with a dog was about the most ludicrous thing he could imagine when sober.

"Sig," he said, "I'm trying to help her learn what things look like. You doubtless do a fine job guiding her around in this world which she cannot see—but she needs to know what it looks like now, and I'm going to show her."

"Then she, will not, need me."

"Of course she will." Render almost laughed. The pathetic thing was here bound so closely to the absurd thing that he could not help it. "I can't restore her sight," he explained. "I'm just going to transfer her some sight-abstractions—sort of lend her my eyes for a short time. Savvy?"

"No," said the dog. "Take mine."

Render turned off the music.

The whole mutie-master relationship might be worth six volumes, he decided, *in German.*

He pointed to the far corner.

"Lie down, over there, like Eileen told you. This isn't going to take long, and when it's all over you're going to leave the same way you came—you leading. Okay?"

Sigmund did not answer, but he turned and moved off to the corner, tail drooping again.

Render seated himself and lowered the hood, the operator's modified version of the ro-womb. He was alone before the ninety white buttons and the two red ones. The world ended in the blackness beyond the console. He loosened his necktie and unbuttoned his collar.

He removed the helmet from its receptacle and checked its leads. Donning it then, he swung the half-mask up over his lower face and dropped the darksheet down to meet with it. He rested his right arm in the sling, and with a single tapping gesture, he eliminated his patient's consciousness.

A Shaper does not press white buttons consciously. He wills conditions. Then deeply-implanted muscular reflexes exert an almost imperceptible pressure against the sensitive arm-sling, which glides into the proper position and encourages an extended finger to move forward. A button is pressed. The sling moves on.

Render felt a tingling at the base of his skull; he smelled fresh-cut grass.

Suddenly he was moving up the great gray alley between the worlds. . . .

After what seemed a long time, Render felt that he was footed on a strange Earth. He could see nothing; it was only a sense of presence that informed him he had arrived. It was the darkest of all the dark nights he had ever known.

He willed that the darkness disperse. Nothing happened.

A part of his mind came awake again, a part he had

not realized was sleeping; he recalled whose world he had entered.

He listened for her presence. He heard fear and anticipation.

He willed color. First, red . . .

He felt a correspondence. Then there was an echo.

Everything became red; he inhabited the center of an infinite ruby.

Orange. Yellow . . .

He was caught in a piece of amber.

Green now, and he added the exhalations of a sultry sea. Blue, and the coolness of evening.

He stretched his mind then, producing all the colors at once. They came in great swirling plumes.

Then he tore them apart and forced a form upon them.

An incandescent rainbow arced across the black sky.

He fought for browns and grays below him. Self-luminescent, they appeared—in shimmering, shifting patches.

Somewhere a sense of awe. There was no trace of hysteria though, so he continued with the Shaping.

He managed a horizon, and the blackness drained away beyond it. The sky grew faintly blue, and he ventured a herd of dark clouds. There was resistance to his efforts at creating distance and depth, so he reinforced the tableau with a very faint sound of surf. A transference from an auditory concept of distance came on slowly then, as he pushed the clouds about. Quickly, he threw up a high forest to offset a rising wave of acrophobia.

The panic vanished.

Render focused his attention on tall trees—oaks and pines, poplars and sycamores. He hurled them about like spears, in ragged arrays of greens and browns and yellows, unrolled a thick mat of morning-moist grass, dropped a series of gray boulders and greenish logs at irregular intervals, and tangled and twined the branches overhead, casting a uniform shade throughout the glen.

The effect was staggering. It seemed as if the entire world was shaken with a sob, then silent.

Through the stillness he felt her presence. He had decided it would be best to lay the groundwork quickly, to set up a tangible headquarters, to prepare a field for operations. He could backtrack later, he could repair and amend the results of the trauma in the sessions yet to come; but this much, at least, was necessary for a beginning.

With a start, he realized that the silence was not a withdrawal. Eileen had made herself immanent in the trees and the grass, the stones and the bushes; she was personalizing their forms, relating them to tactile sensations, sounds, temperatures, aromas.

With a soft breeze, he stirred the branches of the trees. Just beyond the bounds of seeing he worked out the splashing sounds of a brook.

There was a feeling of joy. He shared it.

She was bearing it extremely well, so he decided to extend this scope of the exercise. He let his mind wander among the trees, experiencing a momentary doubling of vision, during which time he saw an enormous hand riding in an aluminum carriage toward a circle of white.

He was beside the brook now and he was seeking her, carefully.

He drifted with the water. He had not yet taken on a form. The splashes became a gurling as he pushed the brook through shallow places and over rocks. At his insistence, the waters became more articulate.

"Where are you?" asked the brook.

Here! Here!

Here!

. . . *and here!* replied the trees, the bushes, the stones, the grass.

"Choose one," said the brook, as it widened, rounded a mass of rock, then bent its way down a slope, heading toward a blue pool.

I cannot, was the answer from the wind.

"You must." The brook widened and poured itself into the pool, swirled about the surface, then stilled itself and reflected branches and dark clouds. "Now!"

Very well, echoed the wood, *in a moment.*

The mist rose above the lake and drifted to the bank of the pool.

"Now," tinkled the mist.

Here, then . . .

She had chosen a small willow. It swayed in the wind; it trailed its branches in the water.

"Eileen Shallot," he said, "regard the lake."

The breezes shifted; the willow bent.

It was not difficult for him to recall her face, her body. The tree spun as though rootless. Eileen stood in the midst of a quiet explosion of leaves; she stared, frightened, into the deep blue mirror of Render's mind, the lake.

She covered her face with her hands, but it could not stop the seeing.

"Behold yourself," said Render.

She lowered her hands and peered downwards. Then she turned in every direction, slowly; she studied herself. Finally:

"I feel I am quite lovely," she said. "Do I feel so because you want me to, or is it true?"

She looked all about as she spoke, seeking the Shaper.

"It is true," said Render, from everywhere.

"Thank you."

There was a swirl of white and she was wearing a belted garment of damask. The light in the distance brightened almost imperceptibly. A faint touch of pink began at the base of the lowest cloudbank.

"What is happening there?" she asked, facing that direction.

"I am going to show you a sunrise," said Render, "and I shall probably botch it a bit—but then, it's my first professional sunrise under these circumstances."

"Where are *you?*" she asked.

"Everywhere," he replied.

"Please take on a form so that I can see you."

"All right."

"Your natural form."

He willed that he be beside her on the bank, and he was.

Startled by a metallic flash, he looked downward. The world receded for an instant, then grew stable once again. He laughed, and the laugh froze as he thought of something.

He was wearing the suit of armor which had stood beside their table in *The Partridge and Scalpel* on the night they met.

She reached out and touched it.

"The suit of armor by our table," she acknowledged, running her fingertips over the plates and the junctures. "I associated it with you that night."

". . . And you stuffed me into it just now," he commented. "You're a strong-willed woman."

The armor vanished and he was wearing his gray-brown suit and looseknit bloodclot necktie and a professional expression.

"Behold the real me." He smiled faintly. "Now, to the sunset. I'm going to use all the colors. Watch!"

They seated themselves on the green park bench which had appeared behind them, and Render pointed in the direction he had decided upon as east.

Slowly, the sun worked through its morning attitudes. For the first time in this particular world it shown down like a god, and reflected off the lake, and broke the clouds, and set the landscape to smoldering beneath the mist that arose from the moist wood.

Watching, watching intently, staring directly into the ascending bonfire, Eileen did not move for a long while, nor speak. Render could sense her fascination.

She was staring at the source of all light; it reflected back from the gleaming coin on her brow, like a single drop of blood.

Render said, "That is the sun, and those are clouds"— and he clapped his hands and the clouds covered the sun and there was a soft rumble overhead—"and that is thunder," he finished.

The rain fell then, shattering the lake and tickling their faces, making sharp striking sounds on the leaves, then soft tapping sounds, dripped down from the branches overhead, soaking their garments and plastering their hair, running down their necks and falling into their eyes, turning patches of brown earth to mud.

A splash of lightning covered the sky, and a second later there was another peal of thunder.

". . . And this is a summer storm," he lectured. "You see how the rain affects the foliage, and ourselves. What you just saw in the sky before the thunderclap was lightning."

". . . Too much," she said. "Let up on it for a moment, please."

The rain stopped instantly and the sun broke through the clouds.

"I have the damnedest desire for a cigarette," she said, "but I left mine in another world."

As she said it one appeared, already lighted, between her fingers.

"It's going to taste rather flat," said Render strangely.

He watched her for a moment, then:

"I didn't give you that cigarette," he noted. "You picked it from my mind."

The smoke laddered and spiraled upward, was swept away.

". . . Which means that, for the second time today, I have underestimated the pull of that vacuum in your mind—in the place where sight ought to be. You are assimilating these new impressions very rapidly. You're even going to the extent of groping after new ones. Be careful. Try to contain that impulse."

"It's like hunger," she said.

"Perhaps we had best conclude this session now."

Their clothing was dry again. A bird began to sing.

"No, wait! Please! I'll be careful. I want to see more things."

"There is always the next visit," said Render. "But I suppose we can manage one more. Is there something you want very badly to see?"

"Yes. Winter. Snow."

"Okay"—the Shaper smiled—"then wrap yourself in that fur-piece . . ."

The afternoon slipped by rapidly after the departure of his patient. Render was in a good mood. He felt emptied and filled again. He had come through the first trial without suffering any repercussions. He decided that he was going to succeed. His satisfaction was greater than his fear. It was with a sense of exhilaration that he returned to working on his speech.

". . . And what is the power to hurt?" he inquired of the microphone.

"We live by pleasure and we live by pain," he answered himself. "Either can frustrate and either can encourage. But while pleasure and pain are rooted in biology, they are conditioned by society: thus are values to be derived. Because of the enormous masses of humanity, hectically changing positions in space everyday throughout the cities of the world, there has come into necessary being a series of totally inhuman controls upon these movements. Every day they nibble their way into new areas—driving our cars, flying our planes, interviewing us, diagnosing our diseases—and I can not ever venture a moral judgment upon these intrusions. They have come necessary. Ultimately, they may prove salutary.

"The point I wish to make, however, is that we are often unaware of our own values. We cannot honestly tell what a thing means to us until it is removed from our life-situation. If an object of value ceases to exist, then the psychic energies which were bound up in it are released. We seek after new objects of value in which to invest—mana, if you like, or libido, if you don't. And no one thing which had vanished during the past three or four or five decades was, in itself, massively significant; and no new thing which came into being during that time is massively malicious toward the people it has replaced or the people it in some manner controls. A society though, is made up of many things, and when these things are changed too rapidly the results are unpredictable. An intense study of mental illness is often quite revealing as to the nature of the stresses in the society where the illness was made. If anxiety-patterns fall into special groups and classes, then something of the discontent of society can be learned from them. Karl Jung pointed out that when consciousness is repeatedly frustrated in a quest for values it will turn its search to the unconscious; failing there, it will proceed to quarry its way into the hypothetical collective unconscious. He noted, in the postwar analyses of ex-Nazis, that the longer they searched for something to erect from the ruins of their lives—having lived through a period of classical iconoclasm, and then seen their new ideals topple as well —the longer they searched, the further back they seemed to reach into the collective unconscious of their people. Their dreams themselves came to take on patterns out of the Teutonic mythos.

"This, in a much less dramatic sense, is happening today. There are historical periods when the group tendency for the mind to turn in upon itself, to turn back, is greater than at other times. We are living in such a period of Quixotism in the original sense of the term. This because the power to hurt, in our time is the power to ignore, to baffle—and it is no longer the exclusive property of human beings—"

A buzz interrupted him then. He switched off the recorder, touched the phone-box.

"Charles Render speaking," he told it.

"This is Paul Charter," lisped the box. "I am headmaster at Dilling."

"Yes?"

The picture cleared. Render saw a man whose eyes were set close together beneath a high forehead. The forehead was heavily creased; the mouth twitched as it spoke.

"Well, I want to apologize again for what happened. It was a faulty piece of equipment that caused—"

"Can't you afford proper facilities? Your fees are high enough."

"It was a *new* piece of equipment. It was a factory defect—"

"Wasn't there anybody in charge of the class?"

"Yes, but—"

"Why didn't he inspect the equipment? Why wasn't he on hand to prevent the fall?"

"He *was* on hand, but it happened too fast for him to do anything. As for inspecting the equipment for factory defects, that isn't his job. Look, I'm very sorry. I'm quite fond of your boy. I can assure you nothing like this will ever happen again."

"You're right, there. But that's because I'm picking him up tomorrow morning and enrolling him in a school that exercises proper safety precautions."

Render ended the conversation with a flick of his finger.

After several minutes had passed he stood and crossed the room partly masked, though not concealed, by a shelf of books. It took only a moment for him to open it and withdraw a jewel box containing a cheap necklace and a framed photograph of a man resembling himself, though somewhat younger and a woman whose upswept hair was dark and whose chin was small, and two youngsters between them—the girl holding the baby in her arms and forcing her bright bored smile on ahead. Render always stared for only a few seconds on such occasions, fondling the necklace, and then he shut the box and locked it away again for many months.

Whump! Whump! went the bass. *Tchg-tchg-tchga-tchg*, the gourds.

The gelatins splayed reds, greens, blues and godawful yellows about the amazing metal dancers.

HUMAN? asked the marquee.

Robots? (immediately below).

COME SEE FOR YOURSELF! (across the bottom, cryptically).

So they did.

Render and Jill were sitting at a microscopic table, thankfully set back against a wall, beneath charcoal caricatures of personalities largely unknown (there being so many personalities among the subcultures of a city of 14 million people). Nose crinkled with pleasure, Jill stared at the present focal point of this particular subculture, occasionally raising her shoulders to ear level to add emphasis to a silent laugh or a small squeal, because the performers were just *too* human—the way the ebon robot ran his fingers along the silver robot's forearm as they parted and passed . . .

Render alternated his attention between Jill and the dancers and a wicked-looking decoction that resembled nothing so much as a small bucket of whisky sours strewn with seaweed (through which the Kraken might at any moment arise to drag some hapless ship down to its doom).

"Charlie, I think they're really people!"

Render disentangled his gaze from her hair and bouncing earrings.

He studied the dancers down on the floor, somewhat below the table area, surrounded by music.

There *could* be humans within those metal shells. If so, their dance was a thing of extreme skill. Though the manufacture of sufficiently light alloys was no problem, it would be some trick for a dancer to cavort so freely—and for so long a period of time, and with such effortless-seeming ease—within a head-to-toe suit of armor, without so much as a grate or a click or a clank.

Soundless . . .

They glided like two gulls; the larger, the color of polished anthracite, and the other, like a moonbeam falling through a window upon a silk-wrapped manikin.

Even when they touched there was no sound—or if there was, it was wholly masked by the rhythms of the band.

Whump-whump! Tchga-tchg!

Render took another drink.

Slowly, it turned into an apache-dance. Render checked his watch. Too long for normal entertainers, he decided. They must be robots. As he looked up again the black robot hurled the silver robot perhaps ten feet and turned his back on her.

There was no sound of striking metal.

Wonder what a setup like that costs? he mused.

"Charlie! There was no sound! How do they do that?"

"Really?" asked Render.

The gelatins were yellow again, then red, then blue, then green.

"You'd think it would damage their mechanisms, wouldn't you?"

The white robot crawled back and the other swiveled his wrist around and around, a lighted cigarette between the fingers. There was laughter as he pressed it mechanically to his lipless faceless face. The silver robot confronted him. He turned away again, dropped the cigarette, ground it out slowly, soundlessly, then suddenly turned back to his partner. Would he throw her again? No . . .

Slowly then, like the great-legged birds of the East, they recommenced their movements, slowly, and with many turnings away.

Something deep within Render was amused, but he was too far gone to ask it what was funny. So he went looking for the Kraken in the bottom of the glass instead.

Jill was clutching his bicep then, drawing his attention back to the floor.

As the spotlight tortured the spectrum, the black robot raised the silver one high above his head, slowly, slowly, and then commenced spinning with her in that position —arms outstretched, back arched, legs scissored—very slowly, at first. Then faster.

Suddenly they were whirling with an unbelievable speed, and the gelatins rotated faster and faster.

Render shook his head to clear it.

They were moving so rapidly that they *had* to fall— human or robot. But they didn't. They were a mandala. They were a gray-form uniformity. Render looked down.

Then slowing, and slower, slower. Stopped.

The music stopped.

Blackness followed. Applause filled it.

When the lights came on again the two robots were standing statue-like, facing the audience. Very, very slowly, they bowed.

The applause increased.

Then they turned and were gone.

Then the music came on and the light was clear again. A babble of voices arose. Render slew the Kraken.

"What d'you think of that?" she asked him.

Render made his face serious and said: "Am I a man

dreaming I am a robot, or a robot dreaming I am a man?" He grinned, then added: "I don't know."

She punched his shoulder gaily at that and he observed that she was drunk.

"I am not," she protested. "Not much, anyhow. Not as much as you."

"Still, I think you ought to see a doctor about it. Like me. Like now. Let's get out of here and go for a drive."

"Not yet, Charlie. I want to see them once more, huh? Please?"

"If I have another drink I won't be able to see that far."

"Then order a cup of coffee."

"Yaagh!"

"Then order a beer."

"I'll suffer without."

There were people on the dance floor now, but Render's feet felt like lead.

He lit a cigarette.

"So you had a dog talk to you today?"

"Yes. Something very disconcerting about that . . ."

"Was she pretty?"

"It was a boy dog. And boy, was he ugly!"

"Silly. I mean his mistress."

"You know I never discuss cases, Jill."

"You told me about her being blind and about the dog. All I want to know is if she's pretty."

"Well . . . yes and no." He bumped her under the table and gestured vaguely. "Well, you know . . ."

"Same thing all the way around," she told the waiter who had appeared suddenly out of an adjacent pool of darkness, nodded, and vanished as abruptly.

"There go my good intentions," sighed Render. "See

how you like being examined by a drunken sot, that's all
I can say."

"You'll sober up fast, you always do. Hippocratics and
all that."

He sniffed, glanced at his watch.

"I have to be in Connecticut tomorrow. Pulling Pete
out of that damned school . . ."

She sighed, already tired of the subject.

"I think you worry too much about him. Any kid can
bust an ankle. It's a part of growing up. I broke my wrist
when I was seven. It was an accident. It's not the school's
fault those things sometimes happen."

"Like hell," said Render, accepting his dark drink from
the dark tray the dark man carried. "If they can't do a
good job I'll find someone who can."

She shrugged.

"You're the boss. All I know is what I read in the papers."

"—And you're still set on Davos, even though you
know you meet a better class of people at Saint Moritz?"
she added.

"We're going there to ski, remember? I like the runs
better at Davos."

"I can't score any tonight, can I?"

He squeezed her hand.

"You always score with me, honey."

And they drank their drinks and smoked their cigarettes and held their hands until the people left the
dance floor and filed back to their microscopic tables, and
the gelatins spun round and round, tinting clouds of
smoke from hell to sunrise and back again, and the bass
went *whump!*

Tchga-tchga!

"Oh, Charlie! Here they come again!"

The sky was clear as crystal. The roads were clean. The snow had stopped.

Jill's breathing was the breathing of a sleeper. The S-7 arced across the bridges of the city. If Render sat very still he could convince himself that only his body was drunk; but whenever he moved his head the universe began to dance about him. As it did so, he imagined himself within a dream, and Shaper of it all.

For one instant this was true. He turned the big clock in the sky backward, smiling as he dozed. Another instant and he was awake again, and unsmiling.

The universe had taken revenge for his presumption. For one renown moment with the helplessness which he had loved beyond helping, it had charged him the price of the lake-bottom vision once again; and as he had moved once more toward the wreck at the bottom of the world—like a swimmer, as unable to speak—he heard, from somewhere high over the Earth, and filtered down to him through the waters above the Earth, the howl of the Fenris Wolf as it prepared to devour the moon; and as this occurred, he knew that the sound was as like to the trump of a judgment as the lady by his side was unlike the moon. Every bit. In all ways. And he was afraid.

III

HE WAS A DOG.

But he was no ordinary dog.

He was driving out into the country, by himself.

Big, a German Shepherd in appearance—except for his head—he sat on his haunches in the front seat, staring out the window at the other cars and at what he could see of the countryside. He passed other cars because he was moving in the high-acceleration lane.

It was a cold afternoon and snow lay upon the fields; the trees wore jackets of ice, and all the birds in the sky and on the ground seemed exceptionally dark.

The dog opened his mouth and his long tongue touched the windowpane and his breath steamed it. His head was larger than any dog's head, excepting perhaps an Irish Wolfhound's. His eyes were deep-set and dark, and his mouth was opened because he was laughing.

He raced on.

The car finally moved across the highway, slowing, entered the extreme righthand lane, and after a time turned into a cutoff. It moved up a country road for several miles, then it turned into a narrow lane and parked itself beneath a tree.

After a moment, the engine stopped and the door opened.

The dog left the car and pushed the door most of the

way shut with his shoulder. When he saw the dome-light go out he turned and walked away into the field, heading toward the woods.

He raised his paws carefully. He examined his footprints.

When he entered the woods he took several deep breaths.

Then he shook himself all over.

He barked a strange, un-doglike bark and began to run.

He ran among the trees, and the rocks, jumped over frozen puddles, small gullies, raced up hills and down slopes, dashed past glassy, rainbow-dotted bushes, moved beside an icy creekbed.

He stopped and panted. He sniffed the air.

He opened his mouth and laughed, a thing he had learned from men.

Then, taking a very deep breath, he threw his head back and howled—a thing he had not learned from men.

In fact, he was not certain where he had learned it.

His howl rolled across the hills and echoed among them like a great horn-note.

His ears pricked upright as he listened to the echoes.

Then he heard an answering howl, which was like, yet not like, his own.

There could be no howl quite like his own, because his voice was not wholly the voice of dogs.

He listened, he sniffed, he howled again.

Again, there came an answer. Nearer, this time . . .

He waited, tasting the breezes for the messages they bore.

It was a dog that came toward him up the hill, rapidly at first, then slowing its pace to a walk. It stopped forty feet away and stared at him. Then it lowered its head.

It was some kind of floppy-eared hound—big, mongrel . . .

He sniffed once more, made a small noise in his throat. The dog bared its teeth.

He moved toward it, and it did not move until he was about ten feet away. Then it turned again and began to draw back.

He stopped.

The dog watched him, carefully, and began to circle. It moved to his leeward side and sniffed the wind.

Finally, he made a noise at the dog, deep down in his throat. It sounded strangely like "Hello."

The dog growled at him. He took a step toward it.

"Good dog," he finally said.

It cocked its head to one side.

"Good dog," he said again.

He took another step toward it, and another. Then he sat down.

". . . Ver-ry good dog," he said.

Its tail twitched, slightly.

He rose and walked up to it. It sniffed him all over. He returned the compliment. Its tail wagged, and it circled around and around him and threw its head back and barked twice.

It moved in an ever-widening circle, occasionally lowering its head to the ground. Then it darted off into the woods, head still lowered.

He approached the place where it had last stood and sniffed at the ground. Then he turned and followed the trail through the trees.

After a few seconds he had caught up with it and they were running side by side.

Then he sped on ahead, and the trail circled and dipped and looped. Finally, it was strong indeed.

A rabbit broke from the cover of a small shrub.

He ran it down and seized it in his huge jaws.

It struggled, so he tossed his head.

Its back made a snapping sound and it ceased its struggles.

Then he held it a moment longer and looked around. The hound came rushing up to him, quivering all over.

He dropped the rabbit at its feet.

The hound looked up at him, expectantly.

He watched it.

It lowered its head and tore at the small carcass. The blood made smoke in the cold air. Stray snowflakes landed upon the dog's brown head.

It chewed and swallowed, chewed and swallowed . . .

Finally, he lowered his own head and tore at the thing. The meat was warm and raw and wild. The dog drew back as he seized upon it, a snarl dying in its throat.

He was not especially hungry, though, so he dropped it and moved away. The dog leapt upon it once more.

After that, they hunted together for several hours.

He always beat the hound to the kill, but he always left it for him to eat.

Altogether, they ran down seven rabbits. The last two they left untouched.

The dog sat down and stared at him.

"Good dog," he told it.

It wagged its tail.

"Bad dog," he told it.

The tail stopped wagging.

"Very bad dog."

Its head fell. It look up at him.

He turned and walked away.

It followed him, tail between its legs.

He stopped and looked back over his shoulder.

The dog cringed.

Then he barked five times and howled.

The ears and tail rose again. It moved up to his side, sniffing at him once more.

He made a laughing noise.

"Good dog," he said.

The tail wagged.

He laughed again.

"Mi-cro, ceph, al-ic, id-i-ot," he said.

The tail continued to wag.

He laughed.

"Good dog, good dog, good dog, good dog, good dog."

It ran in a small circle, lowered its head between its front paws and looked up at him.

He bared his fangs and snarled. Then he lept at it and bit it on the shoulder.

It made a yelping noise and ran away.

"Fool!" he growled. "Fool, fool, fool, fool, fool!"

There was no reply.

He howled again, a sound like that of no other animal on earth.

And then he returned to the car, nosed the door open and climbed inside.

He leaned upon a button on the dashboard and the engine started. The door swung itself all the way open, then slammed. With a paw, he pressed out the necessary coordinates. The car backed out from under the tree, then moved up the lane toward the road.

It hurried back onto the highway and then it was gone.

Somewhere a man was walking.

He could have worn a heavier coat this chill morning, but he was fond of the one with the fur collar.

Hands in his pockets, he walked along the guard

fence. On the other side of the fence the cars roared by.

He did not turn his head.

He could have been in any number of other places, but he chose to be there.

He chose to be walking on this chill morning.

He chose not to care about anything but walking.

The cars sped by and he walked slowly, but steadily.

He did not encounter anyone else on foot.

His collar was turned up, against the wind, but it did not stop all of the cold.

He walked on, and the morning bit him and tugged at his clothing. The day held him, walking, in its infinite gallery, unsigned and unnoticed.

Christmas Eve.

. . . The opposite of New Years:

It is the time of year for family reunions, for Yule logs and trees blazing—for gifts, and for the eating of special foods and the drinking of special drinks.

It is the personal time, rather than the social time; it is the time of focusing upon self and family, rather than society at large; it is the time of rimed windows, star-coated angels, of burning bushes, captured rainbows, of fat Santas with two pairs of trousers (because the young-sters who sit upon their laps are easily awed); and the time of cathedral windows, blizzards, carols, bells, man-ger scenes, season's greetings from those far removed (even if they live but a short distance away), of broad-cast Dickens and holly and candles, of poinsettia and evergreen, of snowbanks, firs, spruces, pines, of the Bible and Nedieval England, of "What Child is This?" and "Oh Little Town of Bethlehem," of the birth and the promise, the light in the darkness; the time, and the time to be, the feeling before the realization, the realization before the happening, the trafficking of red and green, the changing of the year's guard, of tradition, loneliness, sympathy, empathy, sentimentality, singing, faith, hope, charity, love, desire, aspiration, fear, fulfillment, realization, faith, hope, death; a time of the gathering together of stones and the casting away of stones, of embracing, getting, losing, laughing, dancing, mourning, rending, silence, speaking, death, and not speaking. It is a time to break down and a time to build up, a time to plant, and a time to pluck that which is planted . . .

Charles Render and Peter Render and Jill DeVille began a quiet Christmas Eve together.

Render's apartment was set atop a tower of steel and glass. It had about it a certain air of permanency. Books lined the walls, an occasional piece of statuary punctuated the shelves; primitive paintings in primary colors were set in open spaces. Small mirrors, concave and convex (and now framed by boughs of holly), were hung in occasional places.

Greeting cards stood upon the mantelpiece. Potted plants (two in the living room, one in the study, two in the kitchen, and a bedroom shrub) wore tinsel, wore stars. Music flooded the suite.

The punch bowl was a pink jewel in a diamond setting. It held court on the low coffee table of fruitwood, its attendant cups glittering in the diffused light.

It was the time of opening of Christmas presents . . .

Jill turned within hers, swirling it about her like a soft-toothed sawblade.

"Ermine!" she exclaimed. "How grand! How fine! Oh, thank you, dear Shaper!"

Render smiled and blew wreaths of smoke.

The light caught her coat.

"Snow, but warm! Ice, but soft . . ." she said.

"The skins of dead animals," he remarked, "are highly potent tributes to the prowess of the hunter. I hunted them for you, going up and down in the Earth, and to and fro in it. I came upon the finest of white creatures and said, 'Give me your skins,' and they did. Mighty is the hunter, Render."

"I have a thing for you," said she.

"Oh?"

"Here. Here is your gift."

He peeled away the wrappings.

"Cufflinks," he said, "totemic ones. Three faces, one above another—golden. Id, ego, and superego—thus shall I name them, the highest face being the most exalted."

"It is the lowest one that is smiling," said Peter.

Render nodded to his son.

"I did not specify which one was the highest," he told him, "and he is smiling because he has pleasures of his own which the vulgar herd shall never understand."

"Baudelaire?" said Peter.

"Hm," said Render. "Yes, Baudelaire."

". . . Badly misphrased," said his son.

"Circumstance," said Render, "is a matter of time and chance. Baudelaire at Christmas is a matter of something old and something new."

"Sounds like a wedding," said Peter.

Jill flushed, above her snowfield of fur, but Render did not seem to notice.

"Now it is time for you to open your gifts," he said.

"All right."

Peter tore at the wrappings.

"An alchemistry set," he remarked, "just what I've

always wanted—complete with alembics, retorts, bain-marie, and a supply of elixir vitae. Great! Thanks, Miss DeVille."

"Please call me 'Jill.' "

"Sure, Jill. Thanks."

"Open the other one."

"Okay."

He tore away the white, with its holly and bells.

"Fabulous!" he noted. "Other things I've always wanted—something borrowed and something blue: the family album in a blue binding, and a copy of the Render Report for the Senate Sub-committee Hearings on Sociopathic Maladjustment among Government Employees. Also, the complete works of Lofting, Grahame, and Tolkein. Thank you, Dad.—Oh my! There's still more! Tallis, Morely, Mozart, and good dead Bach. Fine sounds to fill my room! Thank you, thank you! What can I give you in return?—Well, lessee . . .

"Howzabout these?" he asked.

He handed his father a package, Jill another.

Render opened his, Jill hers.

"A chess set"—Render.

"A compact"—Jill.

"Thank you"—Render.

"Thank you"—Jill.

"You're both welcome."

"How are you coming with the recorder?" asked Render.

"Give a listen," said Peter.

He assembled his recorder and played.

He played of Christmas and holiness, of evening and blazing star, of warm hearth, wassail, shepherds, kings, light, and the voices of angels.

When he was finished he disassembled the recorder and put it away.

"Very good," said Render.

"Yes—good," said Jill. "Very . . ."

"Thanks."

"How was school?" asked Jill.

"Fine," said Peter.

"Will the change be much of a bother?"

"Not really."

"Why not?"

"Because I'm good. I'm a good student. Dad has trained me well—very well."

"But there will be different instructors . . ."

He shrugged.

"If you know an instructor, then you only know an instructor," he said. "If you know a subject though, you know a subject. I know many subjects."

"Do you know anything about architecture?" she asked suddenly.

"What do you want to know?" he said smiling.

She drew back and glanced away.

"The fact that you ask the question the way you do indicates that you know something about architecture."

"Yes," he agreed, "I do. I've been studying it recently."

"That's all I wanted to know—really . . ."

"Thanks. I'm glad you think I know something."

"Why is it that you know architecture, though? I'm sure it isn't a part of the normal curriculum."

"*Nihil hominum.*" He shrugged.

"Okay—I just wondered." She looked quickly in the direction of her purse. "What do you think of it?" she asked, reaching for her cigarettes.

He smiled.

"What can you think about architecture? It's like the sun: It's big, it's bright, and it's there. That's about all—unless you want to get specific."

She flushed again.

Render lit her cigarette.

"I mean, do you like it?"

"Invariably, if it is old and far away—or, if it is new and I am inside it when it is cold outside. I am utilitarian in matters of physical pleasure and romantic in those pertaining to sensibility."

"God!" said Jill, and looked at Render. "What have you been teaching your son?"

"Everything I can," he replied, "as fast as I can."

"Why?"

"I don't want him to be stepped on someday by something the size of a skyscraper, all stuffed full of facts and modern physics."

"It is not in good taste to speak of people as though they were absent," said Peter.

"True," said Render, "but good taste is not always in good taste."

"You make it sound as though someone owes somebody an apology," he noted.

"That is a matter which the individual must decide for himself, or it is without value."

"In that case," he observed, "I've just decided that I don't owe anybody an apology. If anybody owes me one though, I'll accept it like a gentleman, and in good taste."

Render stood, stared down at his son.

"Peter—" he began.

"May I have some more punch?" asked Jill. "It's quite good, and mine is all gone."

Render reached for the cup.

"I'll get it," said Peter.

He took the cup and stirred the punch with its crystal ladle. Then he rose to his feet, leaning one elbow on the back of his chair.

"Peter!"

He slipped.

The cup and its contents fell into Jill's lap. The contents ran in strawberry tracery through the white fur of her coat. The cup rolled to the sofa, coming to rest in the center of a widening stain.

Peter cried and seized his ankle, sitting down on the floor.

The guest-buzzer sounded.

Render mentioned a long medical term, in Latin. He stooped then and took his son's foot in one hand, his ankle in the other.

"Does this hurt?"

"Yes!"

"*This?*"

"Yes! It hurts all over!"

"How about this?"

"Along the side . . . There!"

Render helped him to his feet, held him balanced on his sound foot, reached for his crutches.

"Come on. Along with me. Dr. Heydell has a hobby-lab in his apartment, downstairs. That fast-cast is coming off. I want to X-ray the foot again."

"No! It's not—"

"What about my coat?" said Jill.

The buzzer sounded again.

"Damn everything!" announced Render, and he pushed the call-dot.

"Yes! Who is it?"

There came a sound of breathing.

Then, "Uh, it's me, boss. Did I pick a bad time?"

"Bennie! No, listen—I didn't mean to snap at you, but all hell's just broken loose. Come on up. By the time you get here things will be normal and unhectic again."

". . . Okay, if you're sure it's all right, that is. I just wanted to stop in for a minute. I'm on my way to somewhere else."

"Sure thing. Here's the door."

He tapped the other circle.

"You stay here and let her in, Jill. We'll be back in a few minutes."

"What about my coat? And the sofa . . . ?"

"All in good time. Don't worry. C'mon, Pete."

He guided him out into the hall, where they entered an elevator and directed it to the sixth floor. On the way down, their elevator sighed past Bennie's, on its way up.

The door clicked. Before it could open though, Render pressed the "Hold" button.

"Peter," he said, "why are you acting like a snotty adolescent?"

Peter wiped his eyes.

"Hell, I'm pre-puberty," he said, "and as for being snotty . . ."

He blew his nose.

Render's hand began to rise, fell back again.

He sighed.

"We'll discuss it later."

He released the "Hold" button and the door slid open.

Dr. Heydell's suite was located at the end of the corridor. A large wreath of evergreen and pine cones hung upon the door, encircling its brass knocker.

Render raised the knocker and let it fall.

From within, there came the faint sounds of Christmas music. After a moment, there was a footfall on the other side, and the door opened.

Dr. Heydell stood before them, looking up from behind thick glasses.

"Well, carolers," he announced in a deep voice. "Come in, Charles, and . . . ?"

"My son, Peter," said Render.

"Glad to meet you, Peter," said Heydell. "Come in and join the party."

He drew the door all the way open and stepped aside. They entered into a blast of Christmas, and Render explained, "We had a little accident upstairs. Peter's ankle was broken a short time ago, and he fell on it again just now. I'd like to use your X-ray to check it out."

"Surely," said the small doctor. "Come this way. Sorry to hear about it."

He led them through his living room, about which seven or eight people were variously situated.

"Merry Christmas!"

"Hi there, Charlie!"

"Merry Christmas, Doc!"

"How's the brain-cleaning business?"

Render raised one hand automatically, nodded in four different directions.

"This is Charles Render. He's in neuroparticipation," Heydell explained to the rest, "and this is his son, Peter. We'll be back in a few minutes. Need my lab."

They passed out of the room, moved two steps into a vestibule. Heydell opened the insulated door to his insulated laboratory. The laboratory had cost him considerable time and expense. It had required the consent of the local building authorities, it had had to subscribe to more than full hospital shielding standards, and it had required the agreement of the apartment management, which in turn had been predicated upon the written consent of all the other tenants. Some of the latter had required economic suasion, Render understood.

They entered the laboratory, and Heydell set his apparatus in operation. He took the necessary pictures and ran them through the speed-dry, speed-develop process.

"Good," he announced, as he studied them. "No more damage, and the fracture is healing nicely."

Render smiled. He noticed that his hands had been shaking.

Heydell slapped him on the shoulder.

"So come on out and try our punch."

"Thanks, Heydell. I believe I will." He always called him by his last name, since they were both Charlies.

They shut down the equipment and left the lab.

Back in the living room, Render shook a few hands and sat down on the sofa with Peter.

He sipped his punch, and one of the men he had only just met, a Dr. Minton, began talking to him.

"So you're a Shaper, eh?"

"That's right."

"I've always wondered about that area. We had a bull-session going back at the hospital, just the other week . . ."

"Oh?"

"Our resident psychiatrist mentioned that neuropy treatments are no more nor less successful than ordinary therapeutic courses."

"I'd hardly consider him in a position to judge—especially if it's Mike Mismire you're talking about, and I think you are."

Dr. Minton spread his hands, palms upward.

"He said he's been collecting figures."

"The change rendered the patient in a neuropy session is a qualitative one. I don't know what he means by 'successful.' The results are successful if you eliminate the patient's problem. There are various ways of doing it—as many as there are therapists—but neuropy is qualitatively superior to something like psychoanalysis because it produces measurable, organic changes. It operates directly upon the nervous system, beneath a patina of real and simulated afferent impulses. It induces desired states of self-awareness and adjusts the neurological foundation to support them. Psychoanalysis and allied areas are purely functional. The problem is less likely to recur if it is adjusted by neuropy."

"Then why don't you use it to cure psychotics?"

"It has been done, a couple times. But it is normally too risky an undertaking. Remember, 'participation' is the key word. Two nervous systems, two minds are involved. It can turn into a reverse-therapy session—anti-neuropy—if the pattern of aberrance is too strong for the operator to control. *His* state of self-awareness is then altered, his neurological underpinnings are readjusted. He becomes psychotic himself, suffering actual organic brain damage."

"It would seem that there'd be some way to cut down on that feedback," said Minton.

"Not yet," Render explained, "there isn't—not without sacrificing some of the operator's effectiveness. They're working on the problem right now in Vienna, but so far the answer seems far away."

"If you find one you can probably go into the more significant areas of mental distress," said Minton.

Render drank his punch. He did not like the stress that the man had laid upon the word 'significant.'

"In the meantime," said Render, after a moment, "we

treat what we *can* treat in the best way we know, and neuropy is certainly the best means known."

"There are those who say that you don't really cure neuroses, but cater to them—that you satisfy patients by giving them little worlds all their own to be neurotic in—vacations from reality, places where they're second in commmand to God."

"That is not the case," said Render. "The things which occur in those little worlds are not necessarily things which please them. They are not near to command at all; the Shaper—or, as you say, God—is. It is a learning experience. You learn by pleasure and you learn by pain. Generally, in these cases, it is more painful than it is pleasurable." He lit a cigarette, accepted another cup of punch.

"So I do not consider the criticism a valid one," he finished.

". . . And it is quite expensive," said Minton.

Render shrugged.

"Did you ever price an Omnichannel Neural Transmission and Receiver outfit?"

"No."

"Do it sometime," said Render.

He listened to a Christmas carol, put out his cigarette, and stood.

"Thanks a lot, Heydell," he said. "I've got to be going now."

"What's the hurry?" asked Heydell. "Stay awhile."

"Like to," said Render, "but there are people upstairs I have to get back to."

"Oh? Many?"

"A couple."

"Bring them down. I was about to set up a buffet, and

82

there's more than enough. I'll feed them and ply them with drinks."

"Well—" said Render.

"Fine!" said Heydell. "Why not just call them from here?"

So he did.

"Peter's ankle is all right," he said.

"Great. Now what about my coat?" asked Jill.

"Forget it for now. I'll take care of it later."

"I tried some lukewarm water, but it's still pinkish . . ."

"Put it back in the box, and don't fool around with it any more! I *said* I'd take care of it."

"Okay, okay. We'll be down in a minute. Bennie brought a gift for Peter, and something for you. She's on her way to her sister's place, but she says she's in no hurry."

"Capital. Drag her down. She knows Heydell."

"Fine." She broke the connection.

Christmas Eve.

. . . The opposite of New Year's:

It is the personal time, rather than the social time; it is the time of focusing upon self and family, rather than society. It is a time of many things: A time to get, and a time to lose; a time to keep, and a time to cast away. It is a time to plant, and a time to pluck up that which is planted . . .

They ate from the buffet. Most of them drank the warm Ronrico and cinnamon and cloves and fruit cocktail and ginger-flavored punch. They talked of plastasac lungs and blood screens and diagnosis by computer, and of the worthlessness of penicillin. Peter sat with his hands folded in his lap: listening, watching. His crutches lay at his feet. Music flooded the room.

Jill sat listening, also.

When Render talked everyone listened. Bennie smiled, took another drink. Playboy doctor or not, when Render talked it was with the voice of a disc jockey and the logic of the Jesuits. Her boss was *known*. Who knew Minton? Who knew Heydell? Other doctors, that's all. Shapers were big-time, and she was his secretary-receptionist. *Everybody* knew of the Shapers. There was nothing controversial about being a heart specialist or a bone man, an anesthesiologist or an internal medicine buff. Her boss was her measure of glory. The other girls always asked her about him, about his magic machine . . . "Electronic Svengalis," that's what *Time* had called them, and Render had gotten three paragraphs, two more than any of the others—excepting Bartelmetz, of course.

The music changed to light classical, to ballet. Bennie felt a year's end nostalgia and she wanted to dance again, as she had once long ago. The season and the company, compounded with the music and the punch and the decorations, made her foot tap, slowly, and turned her mind to memories of a spotlight and a stage filled with color and movement and herself. She listened to the talk.

". . . If you can transmit them and receive them, then you can record them, can't you?" Minton was asking.

"Yes," said Render.

"That's what I thought. Why don't they write more about that angle of the thing?"

"Another five or ten years—perhaps less—and they will. Right now though, the use of playback is restricted to qualified personnel."

"Why?"

"Well"—Render paused to light another cigarette—"to be completely frank, it is to keep the whole area under control until we know more about it. The thing could be exploited commercially—and perhaps with disastrous results—if it were left wide open."

"What do you mean?"

"I mean that I could take a fairly stable person and in his mind construct any sort of dream that you could name, and many that you could not—dreams ranging from violence and sex to sadism and perversion—dreams with a plot, like a total-participation story, or dreams which border upon insanity itself: wish-fulfillment dreams on any subject, cast in any manner. I could even pick a visual arts style, from expressionism to surrealism, if you'd like. A dream of violence in a cubist setting? Like that? Great! You could even be the horse of Guernica. I could set it up. I could record the whole thing and play it back to you, or anyone else, any number of times."

"God!"

"Yes, God. I could make you God, too, if you'd like that—and I could make the Creation last you a full seven days. I control the time-sense, the internal clock, and I can stretch actual minutes into subjective hours."

"Sooner or later this thing will happen, won't it?"

"Yes."

"What will the results be?"

"No one really knows."

"Boss," asked Bennie softly, "could you bring a memory to life again? Could you resurrect something from out of the past and make it live over again in a person's mind, and make it just as though the whole thing was real, all over again?"

Render bit his lip, stared at her strangely.

"Yes," he said, after a long pause, "but it wouldn't

really be a good thing to do. It would encourage living in the past, which is now a nonexistent time. It would be a detriment to mental health. It would encourage regression, reversion, would become another means of neurotic escape into the past."

The *Nutcracker Suite* finished, the sounds of *Swan Lake* filled the room.

"Still," she said, "I should like so to be the swan again . . ."

She rose slowly and executed a few clumsy steps—a hefty, tipsy swan in a russet dress.

She flushed then and sat down quickly. Then she laughed and everyone joined her.

"Where would *you* like to be?" Minton asked Heydell.

The small doctor smiled.

"Back on a certain weekend during the summer of my third year in med school," he said. "Yes, I'd wear out that tape in a week. How about you, son?" he asked Peter.

"I'm too young to have any good memories yet," Peter replied. "What about you, Jill?"

"I don't know . . . I think I'd like being a little girl again," she said, "and having Daddy—I mean, my father—read to me on a Sunday afternoon, in the wintertime."

She glanced at Render then.

"And you, Charlie?" she asked. "If you were being unprofessional for a moment, what would your moment be?"

"This one," he said, smiling. "I'm happy right where I am, in the present, where I belong."

"Are you, are you really?"

"Yes!" he said, and he took another cup of punch.

Then he laughed.

"Yes, I really am."

A soft snore came from beside him. Bennie had dozed off.

And the music went round and round, and Jill looked from father to son and back again. Render had replaced the fastcast on Peter's ankle. The boy was yawning now. She studied him. What would he be in ten years? Or fifteen? A burnt-out prodigy? Master of some as yet unexploited quantity?

She studied Peter, who was watching his father.

". . . But it could be a genuine art form," Minton was saying, "and I don't see how censorship . . ."

She studied Render.

". . . A man does not have a *right* to be insane," he was saying, "any more than he has a right to commit suicide . . ."

She touched his hand and he jumped, as though awakened from a doze, jerking his hand away.

"I'm getting tired," she said. "Would you take me home now?"

"In a while," he replied, nodding. "Let's let Bennie catch a little more shuteye first, though," and he turned back to Minton.

Peter turned to her and smiled.

Suddenly, she was really very tired.

Always before, she had liked Christmas.

Across from her, Bennie continued to snore, a faint smile occasionally flickering across her features.

Somewhere, she was dancing.

Somewhere, a man named Pierre was screaming, possibly because he was no longer a man named Pierre.

Me? I'm Vital, like it says in *Time*, your weekly. Move in for a close pan-shot, Charlie. No, don't *you* pan! *My* pan. See? There. The expression always comes to the man on the cover after he's read the article behind the cover. It's too late then, though. Well, they mean well, but you know . . . Send a boy to bring me a pitcher of water and a basin, okay? 'Death of the Bit,' that's what they called it. Said a man could work the same bit for years, moving about a vast and complex sociological structure known as 'the circuit,' and letting the thing fall upon new and virgin ears on each occasion. Oh, living death! Worldwide telecommunications pushed this wheelchair downhill countless elections ago. It bounces now among the rocks of Limbo. We are come upon a new and glorious and vital era. . . . So, all you people out there in Helsinki and Tierra del Fuego, tell me if you've heard this one before: It concerns an old-time comic with what they called a 'bit.' One night he did a broadcast performance, and as was his wont he did his bit. Good and pat and solid was his bit, and full of point, balance, and antithesis. Unfortunately, he was out of a job after that, because everyone then knew this bit. Despairing, scraping himself with potsherds, he mounted the rail of the nearest bridge. About to cast himself down into the dark and flowing death-symbol below, he was suddenly halted by a voice. 'Do not cast yourself down into the dark and flowing death-symbol below,' said the voice. 'Throw away your potsherds and come down from that rail.' Turning about, he saw a strange creature—that is to say, ugly—all in white, regarding him with a near-toothless smile. 'Who are you, oh strange, smiling creature all in white?' he asked. 'I am an Angel of Light,' she replied, 'and I am come to stop you from killing yourself.' He shook his head. 'Alas,' said he, 'but I must kill myself, for my bit is all used up.' Then she raised a palm, thus . . . 'Despair not,' she said. 'Despair not, for we Angels of

Light can work miracles. I can render unto thee more
bits than can possibly be used in the brief, wearisome
span of mortal existence.' Then, 'Pray,' said he, 'tell me
what I must do to effect this miraculous occurrence.'
—'Sleep with me,' replied the Angel of Light. 'Is this not
somewhat irregular and unangelic?' he asked. 'Not at all,'
said she. 'Read the Old Testament carefully and you will be
surprised at what you learn of angelic relations.'—'Very
well,' he agreed, throwing away his potsherds. And they
went away and he did his other bit, despite the fact that
she was scarcely the most comely among the Daughters
of Light. The following morning he arose eagerly, tapped
the skin he had touched to love and cried, 'Awake!
Awake! It is time for you to render me my perpetual
supply of bits!' She opened one eye and stared up at him.
'How long have you been doing your bit?' she asked him.
'Thirty years,' said he. 'And how old does that make
you?' she inquired. 'Uh—forty-five,' he replied. She
yawned then and smiled. 'Is that not rather old to be
believing in Angels of Light?' she asked. Then he went off
and did his other bit, of course. . . . Now let me have a
little soothing music, huh? That's good. Really makes you
wince, doesn't it—You know why?—Where do you hear
soothing music these days, anyhow?—well, in dentists'
offices, and banks and stores and places like that where
you always have to wait real long to get served. You hear
soothing music while you're undergoing all this massive
trauma. The result of this? Soothing music is now about
the most unsoothing thing in the world. It always makes
me hungry, too. They play it in all those restaurants
where they're slow in waiting on you. You wait on them,
that's what it is—and they play you this damn soothing
music. Well. . . . Where's that boy with the pitcher and
the basin, anyhow? I want to wash my hands. . . . You

hear about the AF man who made it out to Centaurus? He discovered a race of humanoid creatures and got to work learning their customs, folkways, mores and taboos. Finally, he touched upon the question of reproduction. A delicate young female then took him by the hand and led him to a large factory where Centaurians were being assembled. Yes, that's right—torsos were going by on conveyor belts, and balls screwed in, brains dropped into the skulls, fingernails inserted, organs stuffed in, and so on. He voiced his amazement at this, and she said, 'Why? How do you do it on Earth?' Then, taking her by her delicate hand, he said, 'Come with me over yonder hill and I shall demonstrate.' During the course of his demonstration she began to laugh hysterically. 'What is the matter?' he inquired. 'Why are you laughing at me?'—'This,' she replied, 'is the way we make cars.' . . . Fade me, Babes, and sell some toothpaste!

". . . Aiee! That I, Orpheus, should be torn into pieces by such as ye! But in a sense, perhaps, it *is* fitting. Come then, ye Corybantes, and work your will upon the singer!"

Darkness. A scream.

Silence . . .

Applause!

She always came early and entered alone; and she always sat in the same seat.

She sat in the tenth row, on the righthand aisle, and her only real trouble was at intermission time: she could never tell when someone wanted to get past her.

She arrived early, and she remained until the theater was silent.

She loved the sound of a trained voice, which was why she preferred British actors to Americans.

She liked musicals, not so much because she liked the music, but because she liked the feeling of voices which throbbed. This is also why she was fond of verse plays.

She liked the Elizabethans, but she did not like *King Lear*.

She was stimulated by the Greek plays, but she could not bear *Oedipus Rex*.

She did not like *The Miracle Worker*, nor *The Light That Failed*.

She wore tinted glasses, but not dark ones. She did not carry a cane.

On a certain night, before the curtain went up for the final act, a spotlight pierced the darkness. A man stepped into the hole it made and asked, "Is there a doctor in the house?"

No one answered.

"It is an emergency," he said. "If there *is* a doctor here, will you please visit the office in the main lobby, immediately?"

He looked around the theater as he spoke, but no one moved.

"Thank you," he said, and left the stage.

Her head had jerked toward the circle of light when it appeared.

After the announcement, the curtain was rung up and the movement and the voices began again.

She waited, listening. Then she stood and moved up the aisle, brushing the wall with her fingertips.

When she reached the lobby she stopped and stood there.

"May I help you, Miss?"

"Yes, I'm looking for the office."

"It's right there, to your left."

She turned and moved to her left, her hand extended slightly before her.

When she touched the wall she moved her hands quickly until they struck a door jamb.

She knocked upon the door and waited.

"Yes?" It opened.

"You need a doctor?"

"You're a doctor?"

"That's right."

"Quick! This way!"

She followed the man's footsteps inside and up a corridor that paralleled the aisles.

Then she heard him climb seven stairs and she followed him up them.

They came to a dressing room and she followed him inside.

"Here he is."

She followed the voice.

"What happened?" she asked, reaching out.

She touched a man's body.

There was a gurgling rasp and a series of breathless coughs.

"Stagehand," said the man. "I think he's choking on a piece of taffy. He's always chewing the stuff. There seems to be something back up in his throat. Can't get at it, though."

"Have you sent for an ambulance?"

"Yes. But look at him—he's turning blue! I don't know if they'll be here in time."

She dropped the wrist, forced the head backwards. She felt down along the inside of the throat.

"Yes, there is some sort of obstruction. I can't get at it either. Get me a short, sharp knife—a sterile one—fast!"

"Yes, ma'am, right away!"

He left here there alone.

She felt the pulses of the carotids. She placed her hands on the heaving chest. She pushed the head further backwards and reached down the throat again.

A minute went by, and part of another.

There came a sound of hurrying footsteps.

"Here you are . . . We washed the blade in alcohol . . ."

She took the knife in her hands. In the distance there was the sound of an ambulance siren. She could not be sure though, that they would make it in time.

So she examined the blade with her fingertips. Then she explored the man's neck.

She turned, slightly, toward the presence she felt beside her.

"I don't think you had better watch this," she stated. "I am going to do an emergency tracheotomy. It's not a pretty sight."

"Okay. I'll wait outside."

Footsteps, going away . . .

She cut.

There was a sigh. There was a rushing of air.

There was wetness . . . a bubbling sound.

She moved the head. When the ambulance arrived at the stage door, her hands were steady again, because she knew that the man was going to live.

". . . Shallot," she told the doctor, "Eileen Shallot, State Psych."

"I've heard of you. Aren't you . . . ?"

"Yes, I am, but it's easier to read people than Braille."

"I see—yes. Then we can get in touch with you at State?"

"Yes."

"Thank you, Doctor. Thank you," said the manager.

She returned to her seat for the rest of the play.

After the final curtain, she sat there until the theater was emptied.

Sitting there, she still sensed the stage.

To her, the stage was a focal point of sound, rhythm, the sense of movement, some nuances of light and dark—but not of color: It was the center of a special kind of brilliance for her: It was the place of the *pathema-mathema-poeima* pulse, of the convulsion of life through the cycle of passions and perceptions; the place where those capable of noble suffering suffered nobly, the place where the clever Frenchmen wove their comedies of gossamer among the pillars of Idea; the place where the black poetry of the nihilists whored itself for the price of admission from those it mocked, the place where blood was spilt and cries were uttered and songs were sung, and where Apollo and Dionysius smirked from the wings, where Arlecchino perpetually tricked Capitano Spezzafer out of his trousers. It was the place where any action could be imitated, but where there were really only two things behind all actions: the happy and the sad, the comic and the tragic—that is, love and death—the two things which named the human condition; it was the place of the heroes and the less-than-heroes; it was the place that she loved, and she saw there the only man whose face she knew, walking, symbol-studded, upon its surface. . . . To take up arms against a sea of troubles, ill-met by moonlight, and by opposing end them—who hath called forth the mutinous winds, and 'twixt the green sea and the azured vault set roaring war—for those are pearls that were his eyes. . . . What a piece of work is a man! Infinite in faculty, in form and in moving!

She knew him in all his roles, who could not yet exist

without an audience. He was Life.

He was the Shaper . . .

He was the Maker and the Mover.

He was greater than heroes.

A mind may hold many things. It learns. It cannot teach itself not to think, though.

Emotions remain the same, qualitatively, throughout life; the stimuli to which they respond are subject to quantitative variations, but the feelings are stock in trade.

This why the theater survives: it is cross-cultural; it contains the North Pole and the South Pole of the human condition; the emotions fall like iron filings within its field.

A mind cannot teach itself not to think, but feelings fall into destined patterns.

He was her theater . . .

He was the poles of the world.

He was all actions.

He was not the imitation of actions, but the actions themselves.

She knew he was a very capable man named Charles Render.

She felt he was the Shaper.

A mind may hold many things.

But he was more than any one thing:

He was every.

. . . She felt it.

When she stood to leave, her heels made echoes across the emptied dark.

As she moved up the aisle, the sounds returned to her and returned to her.

She was walking through an emptied theater, away from an emptied stage. She was alone.

At the head of the aisle, she stopped.

Like distant laughter, ended by a sudden slap, there was silence.

She was neither audience nor player now. She was alone in a dark theater.

She had cut a throat and saved a life.

She had listened tonight, felt tonight, applauded tonight.

Now, again, it was all gone away, and she was alone in a dark theater.

She was afraid.

The man continued to walk along the highway until he reached a certain tree. He stood, hands in his pockets, and stared at it for a long while. Then he turned and headed back in the direction from which he had come.

Tomorrow was another day.

"Oh, sorrow-crowned love of my life, why hast thou forsaken me? Am I not fair? I have loved thee long, and all the places of silence know my wailings. I have loved thee beyond myself, and I suffer for it. I have loved thee beyond life with all its sweetness, and the sweetnesses have turned to cloves and to almonds. I am ready to leave this my life for thee. Why shouldst thou depart in the greatwinged, manylegged ships over the sea, bearing with thee thy Lares and Penates, and I here alone? I shall make me a fire, to burn. I shall make me a fire—a conflagration to incinerate time and to burn away the spaces that separate us. I would be with thee always. I shall not go gently and silent into that holocaust, but wailing. I am no ordinary maiden, to pine away my life and to die, dark-eyed and sallow. For I am of the blood of the Princes of the Earth, and my arm is as the arm of a man's in the battle. My upraised sword smites the helm of my foe and he falls down before it. I have never been subdued, my lord. But my eyes are sick of weeping, and my tongue of crying out. To make me to see thee, and then to never see thee again is a crime beyond expiation. I cannot forgive my love, nor thee. There was a time when I laughed at the songs of love and the plaints of the maidens by the riverside. Now is my laughter drawn, as an arrow from a wound, and I am myself without thee and alone. Forgive me not, love, for having loved thee. I want to fuel a fire with memory and my hopes. I want to set to burning my already burning thoughts of thee, to lay thee like a poem upon a campfire, to burn thy rhythmic utterance to ash. I loved thee, and thou hast departed. Never again will I see thee in this life, hear again the music of thy voice, feel again the thunder of thy touch. I loved thee, and I am forsaken and alone. I loved thee, and my words fell upon ears that were deaf and my self upon eyes that saw not. Am I not fair, oh winds of the Earth, who wash me over, who stoke these, my fires? Why then hast thou forsaken me, oh life of the heart in my breast? I go now to the flame my father, to better be received. In all the passes of loving, there will never be another such as thee. May the gods bless thee and sustain thee, oh light, and may their judgment not come too heavy upon thee for this thing thou hast done. Aeneas, I burn for thee! Fire, be my last love!"

There was applause as she swayed within the lighted circle and fell. Then the room was darkened.

A moment later the light was restored, and the other members of the Act a Myth Club rose and came forward to congratulate her on her perceptive interpretation. They discussed the significance of the folk-motif, from the *suttee* to the immolation of Brunhilde. Good, basic—fire—

they decided. "Fire . . . my last love"—good: Eros and Thanatos in a final cleansing burst of flame.

After they had used up their appreciation, a small, stooped man and his birdlike, birdtracked wife moved to the center of the room.

"Heloise and Abelard," the man announced.

A respectful silence gathered about them.

A beefy man in his middle-forties moved to his side, face glazed with perspiration.

"My chief castrater," said Abelard.

The big man smiled and bowed.

"Now, let us begin . . ."

There was a single clap and darkness fell.

Like deep-burrowing, mythological worms, power lines, pipelines, and pneumatic tubes stretch themselves across the continent. Pulsing, peristalsis-like, they drink of the Earth and the thunderbolt. They take oil and electricity and water and coal-wash and small parcels and large packages and letters into themselves. Passing through them, beneath the Earth, these things are excreted at their proper destinations, and the machines who work in these places take over from there.

Blind, they sprawl far away from the sun; without taste, the Earth and the thunderbolt go undigested; without smell or hearing, the Earth is their rock-filled prison. They only know what they touch; and touching is their constant function.

Such is the deep-buried joy of the worm.

Render had spoken with the staff psychologist and had inspected the physical education equipment at the new school. He had also inspected the students' quarters and had been satisfied.

Now, though, as he left Peter once again at the place of education, he felt somehow dissatisfied. He was not certain why. Everything had seemed in as good order as it had been when first he had visited. Peter had seemed in high spirits, too. Exceptionally high spirits.

He returned to his car and drifted out onto the highway—that great rootless tree whose branches covered two continents (and once the Bering Bridgeway was completed would enfold the world, saving only Australia, the polar icecaps, and islands)—he wondered, and wondering, he found no answer to his discontent.

Should he call Jill and ask about her cold? Or was she still angry over her coat and the Christmas that had accompanied it?

His hands fell into his lap, and the countryside jumped up and down around him as he moved through the ranks of the hills.

His hand twitched toward the panel once more.

"Hello?"

"Eileen, Render here. I didn't get to call you when it happened, but I heard about that tracheotomy you performed at the Play House . . ."

"Yes," she said, "good thing I was handy—me and a sharp knife. Where are you calling from?"

"My car. I just left Peter at school. On my way back now."

"Oh? How is he? His ankle . . . ?"

"Fine. We had a little scare there at Christmas, but nothing came of it.—Tell me how it happened at the Play House, if it doesn't bother you."

"Blood bother a doctor?" She laughed softly. "Well, it was late, right before the last act . . ."

Render leaned back and smiled, lit a cigarette, listened.

Outside, the country settled down to a smooth plain and he coasted across it like a bowling ball, right in the groove all the way to the pocket.

He passed a walking man.

Beneath high wires and above buried cables, he was walking again, beside a great branch of the road-tree, walking through snow-specked air and broadcast power.

Cars sped by, and a few of their passengers saw him.

His hands were in the pockets of his jacket and his head was low, because he looked at nothing. His collar was turned up and heaven's melting contributions, the snowflakes, were collected on the brim of his hat.

He wore rubbers. The ground was wet and a little muddy.

He trudged on, a stray charge within the field of a great generator.

". . . Dinner tonight at the P & S?"

"Why not?" said Render.

"Say eight?"

" 'Eight.' Tally-ho!"

Some of them dropped down out of the sky, but mainly they came spinning in off the roads . . .

The cars released their people onto platforms within the great car-hives. The air-taxis set theirs free in landing areas, near to the kiosks of the underground beltway.

But whatever the means by which they arrived, the people toured Exhibit Hall on foot.

The building was octagonal, its roof an inverted soup

bowl. Eight nonfunctional triangles of black stone provided decoration at each corner, without.

The soup bowl was a selective filter. Right now, it was sucking all the blue out of the gray evening and was glowing faintly on the outside—whiter than all the dirty snows of yesterday. Its ceiling was a cloudless summer sky at eleven o'clock in the A.M., without a sun to mar its Morning Glory frosting.

The people flowed beneath this sky, passed among the exhibits, moved like a shallow stream through a place of rocks.

They moved in ripples and random swirlings. They eddied; they churned, bubbled, babbled. Occasionally, there was a sparkle . . .

They poured steadily from the parked machines beyond the blue horizon.

After they had run their course, they completed the circuit by returning to the metal clouds which had borne them to the running.

It was Outward that they passed.

Outward was the Air Force-sponsored Exhibit which had been open for the past two weeks, twenty-four hours a day, and which had drawn spectators from all over the world.

Outward was a survey of Man's achievements in Space.

Heading Outward was a two-star general, with a dozen colonels, eighteen lieutenant colonels, many majors, numerous captains, and countless lieutenants on his staff. Nobody ever saw the general, excepting the colonels and the people from Exhibits, Incorporated. Exhibits, Incorporated owned Exhibit Hall, there by the spaceport, and they set things up in good taste for all the exhibitionists who employed them.

First, to the right, as you entered Toadstool Hall (as it had been dubbed by some Vite), was the Gallery.

In the Gallery were the mural-sized photos that a spectator could almost walk off into, losing himself in the high, slender mountains behind Moonbase III (which looked as if they would sway in the wind, were there any wind to sway them); or wander through the bubble-cap of that undermoon city, perhaps running a hand along one of the cold lobes of the observational cerebrum and feeling its rapid thoughts clicking within; or, passing by, enter that rusty desert beneath the greenish sky, cough once or twice, spit bloody spittle, circle the towering walls of the above-ground Port Complex—bluegray, monolithic, built upon the ruins of God knows what— and enter into that fortress where men move like ghosts in a Martian department store, feel the texture of those glassite walls, and make some of the soft and only noises in the whole world; or pass across Mercury's Acre of Hell in the cool of the imagination, tasting the colors— the burning yellow, the cinnamon and the orange—and come to rest at last in Big Ice Box, where Frost Giant battles Fire Wight, and where each compartment is sealed and separately maintained—as in a submarine or transport rocket, and for the same, basic reason; or stroll on out in the direction of the Outer Five, where the hero is heat and cold the villain, stand there in a frosted oven beneath a mountain, hands in pockets, and count the colored streaks in the walls like opals, see the sun as a brilliant star, shiver, exhale vapors, and agree that these are all very wonderful places to have circling about the sun, and nice pictures, too.

After the Gallery were the Grav-rooms, to which one might climb by means of a stairway smelling of fresh-cut

lumber. At the top, one might select the grav one wished
—Moon-weight, Mars-weight. Merc-weight—and ride
back to the floor of the Hall on a diminishing cushion of
air, elevator-like, knowing for a moment the feeling of
weight personal carried on the chosen world impersonal.
The platform drops down, the landing is muffled . . .
Like falling into hay, like falling into a feather bed.

Next, there was a waist-high rail—brass. It went around
the Fountain of the Worlds.

Lean over, look down . . .

Scooped out of the light was a bottomless pool of
black . . .

It was an orrery.

In it, the worlds swung on magnetic lines, glowing.
They moved around a burning beachball of a sun; the
distance to the outer ones was scaled down, and they
shone frostily, palely, through the murk; the Earth was
emerald, turquoise; Venus was milky jade; Mars, an orange sherbet; Mercury, butter, Galliano, breadcrust,
fresh-baked.

Food and riches hung in the Fountain of the Worlds.
Those who hungered and lusted leaned on the brass rail
and stared. Such is the stuff dreams are made of.

The others looked and passed by, going on to see the
full-sized reconstruction of the decompression chamber
of Moonbase I, or to hear the valve manufacturer's representative give little-known facts concerning the con-
struction of the pressure-locks and the power of the air
pumps. (He was a short, red-haired man who knew
many statistics.) Or they rode across the Hall in the cars
of the over-head-suspension monorail. Or they saw the
20-minute *Outward—With Stops At Spots* film, which
was so special as to feature a live narrator rather than

soundtrack. They mounted freshly-heaped wall-cliffs in scaleboats, and they operated the pincers of the great claw-cans, used for off-Earth strip-mining.

Those who hungered stayed longer, though, in one place.

They stayed longer, laughed less.

They were the part of the flow which formed pools, sparkled . . .

"Interested in heading out some day?"

The boy turned his head, shifted on his crutches.

He regarded the lieutenant colonel who had addressed him. The officer was tall. Tanned hands and face, dark eyes, a small moustache and a narrow, brown pipe, smoldering, were his most prominent features, beyond his crisp and tailored uniform.

"Why?" asked the boy.

"You're about the right age to be planning your future. Careers have to be mapped out pretty far in advance. A man can be a failure at thirteen if he doesn't think ahead."

"I've read the literature . . ."

"Doubtless. Everyone your age has. But now you're seeing samples—and mind you, they're *only* samples—of the actuality. That's the big, new frontier out there—the great frontier. You can't know the feeling just from reading the booklets."

Overhead, the monorail-car rustled on its way across the Hall. The officer indicated it with his pipe.

"Even *that* isn't the same as riding the thing over a Grand Canyon of ice," he noted.

"Then it is a deficiency on the part of the people who write the booklets," said the boy. "Any human experience should be describable and interpretable—by a good enough writer."

The officer squinted at him.

"Say that again, sonny."

"I said that if your booklets don't say what you want them to say, it's not the fault of the material."

"How old are you?"

"Ten."

"You seem pretty sharp for your age."

The boy shrugged, lifted one crutch and pointed it in the direction of the Gallery.

"A good painter could do you fifty times the job that those big, glossy photos do."

"They are very good photos."

"Of course, they're perfect. Expensive too, probably. But any of those scenes by a real artist could be priceless."

"No room out there for artists yet. Ground-breakers go first, culture follows after."

"Then why don't you change things and recruit a few artists? They might be able to help you find a lot more ground-breakers."

"Hm," said the officer, "that's an angle. Want to walk around with me some? See more of the sights?"

"Sure," said the boy. "Why not? 'Walk' isn't quite the proper verb, though . . ."

He swung into step beside the officer and they moved about the exhibits.

The scaleboats did a wall crawl to their left, and the claw-cans snapped.

"Is the design of those things really based on the structure of a scorpion's pincers?"

"Yes," said the officer. "Some bright engineer stole a

trick from Nature. *That* is the kind of mind we're interested in recruiting."

The boy nodded.

"I've lived in Cleveland. Down on the Cuyahoga River they use a thing called a Hulan Conveyor to unload the oreboats. It is based on the principle of the grasshopper's leg. Some bright young man with the sort of mind you're interested in recruiting was lying in his back yard one day, pulling the legs off grasshoppers, and it hit him: 'Hey,' he said, 'there might be some use to all this action.' He took apart some more grasshoppers and the Hulan Conveyer was born. Like you say, he stole a trick that Nature was wasting on things that just hop around in the fields, chewing tobacco and being pesty. My father once took me on a boat trip up the river and I saw the things in operation. They're great metal legs with claws at the end, and they make the most godawful unearthly noise I ever heard—like the ghosts of all the tortured grasshoppers. I'm afraid I don't have the kind of mind you're interested in recruiting."

"Well," said the officer, "it seems that you might have the other kind."

"What other kind?"

"The kind you were talking about: The kind that will see and interpret, the kind that will tell the people back home what it's really like out there."

"You'd take me on as a chronicler?"

"No, we'd have to take you on as something else. But that shouldn't stop you. How many people were drafted for the World Wars for the purpose of writing war novels? How many war novels were written? How many good ones? There *were* quite a few, you know. You could plan your background to that end."

"Maybe," said the boy.

They walked on.

"Come this way?" asked the officer.

The boy nodded and followed him out into a corridor and then into an elevator. It closed its door and asked them where they wished to be conveyed.

"Sub-balc," said the lieutenant colonel.

There was scarcely a sensation of movement, then the doors opened again. They stepped out onto the narrow balcony which ran around the rim of the soup bowl. It was glassite-enclosed and dimly lit.

Below them lay the pens and a part of the field.

"There will be several vehicles lifting off shortly," said the officer. "I want you to watch them, to see them go up on their wheels of fire and smoke."

" 'Wheels of fire and smoke,' " said the boy, smiling. "I've seen that phrase in lots of your booklets. Real poetic, yes sir."

The officer did not answer him. None of the towers of metal moved.

"These don't really go out, you know," he finally said. "They just convey materials and personnel to the stations in orbit. The real big ships never land."

"Yes, I know. Did a guy really commit suicide on one of your exhibits this morning?"

"No," said the officer, not looking at him, "it was an accident. He stepped into the Mars Grav-room before the platform was in place or the air cushion built up. Fell down the shaft."

"Then why isn't that exhibit closed?"

"Because all the safety devices are functioning properly. The warning light and the guard rail are both working all right."

"Then why did you call it an accident?"

"Because he didn't leave a note. —There! Watch now,

that one is getting ready to lift!" He pointed with his pipe.

A blizzard of vapors built up around the base of one of the steel stalagmites. A light was born in its heart. Then the burning was beneath it, and waves of fumes splashed across the field, broke, rose high into the air.

But not quite so high as the ship.

. . . Because it was moving now.

Almost imperceptibly, it had lifted itself above the ground. Now, though, the movement could be noted.

Suddenly, with a great gushing of flame, it was high in the air, darting against the gray.

It was a bonfire in the sky, then a flare; then it was a star, rushing away from them.

"There is nothing quite like a rocket in flight," said the officer.

"Yes," said the boy. "You're right."

"Do you want to follow it?" said the man. "Do you want to follow that star?"

"Yes," said the boy. "Someday I will."

"My own training was pretty hard, and the requirements are even tougher these days."

They watched two more ships lift off.

"When was the last time you were out, yourself?" asked the boy.

"It's been awhile . . ." said the man.

"I'd better be going now. I've got a paper to write for school."

"Let me give you some of our new booklets first."

"Thanks, I've got them all."

"Okay, then . . . Good night, fella."

"Good night. Thanks for the show."

The boy moved back toward the elevator. The officer

remained on the balcony, staring out, staring up, holding onto his pipe which had gone out.

The light and twisted figures, struggling . . .

Then darkness.

"Oh, the steel! The pain as the blades enter! I am many mouths, all of them vomiting blood!"

Silence.

Then comes the applause.

IV

". . . THE PLAIN, the direct, and the blunt. This is Winchester Cathedral," said the guidebook. "With its floor-to-ceiling shafts, like so many huge treetrunks, it achieves a ruthless control over its spaces: the ceilings are flat; each bay, separated by those shafts, is itself a thing of certainty and stability. It seems, indeed, to reflect something of the spirit of William the Conqueror. Its disdain of mere elaboration and its passionate dedication to the love of another world would make it seem, too, an appropriate setting for some tale out of Mallory . . ."

"Observe the scalloped capitals," said the guide. "In their primitive fluting they anticipated what was later to become a common motif . . ."

"Faugh!" said Render—softly though, because he was in a group inside a church.

"Shh!" said Jill (Fotlock—that was her real last name) DeVille.

But Render was impressed as well as distressed.

Hating Jill's hobby, though, had become so much of a reflex with him that he would sooner have taken his rest seated beneath an oriental device which dripped water on his head than to admit he occasionally enjoyed walking through the arcades and the galleries, the passages and the tunnels, and getting all out of breath climbing up the high twisty stairways of towers.

So he ran his eyes over everything, burnt everything down by shutting them, then built the place up again out of the still smoldering ashes of memory, all so that at a later date he would be able to repeat the performance, offering the vision to his one patient who could see only in this manner. This building he disliked less than most. Yes, he would take it back to her.

The camera in his mind photographing the surroundings, Render walked with the others, overcoat over his arm, his fingers anxious to reach after a cigarette. He kept busy ignoring his guide, realizing this to be the nadir of all forms of human protest. As he walked through Winchester he thought of his last two sessions with Eileen Shallot.

He wandered with her again.

Where the panther walks to and fro on the limb overhead . . .

They wandered.

Where the buck turns furiously at the hunger. .

They had stopped when she held the backs of her hand to her temples, fingers spread wide, and looked sideways at him, her lips parted as if to ask a question.

"Antlers," he had said.

She nodded, and the buck approached.

She felt its antlers, rubbed its nose, examined its hooves.

"Yes," she'd said, and it had turned and walked away and the panther had leapt down upon its back and torn at its neck.

She watched as it bayonetted the cat twice, then died. The panther tore at its carcass and she looked away.

Where the rattlesnake suns his flabby length on a rock . . .

She watched it coil and strike, coil and strike, three times. Then she felt its rattles.

She turned back to Render.

"Why *these* things?"

"More than the idyllic must you know," he had said, and he pointed.

. . . *Where the alligator in his tough pimples sleeps by the bayou.*

She touched the plated hide. The beast yawned. She studied its teeth, the structure of its jaw.

Insects buzzed about her. A mosquito settled on her arm and began to sting her. She slapped at it and laughed.

"Do I pass?" she asked.

Render smiled, nodded.

"You hold up well."

He clapped his hands, and the forest was gone, and the swamp was gone.

They stood barefoot on stirring sands, and the sun and its folding ghost came down to them from the surface of the water high above their heads. A school of bright fish swam between them, and the seaweed moved back and forth, polishing the currents that passed.

Their hair rose and moved about like the seaweed, and their clothing stirred. Whorled, convoluted and twisted, pink and blue and white and red and brown, trails of seashells lay before them, leading past walls of coral, heaps of seasmoothed stone, and the toothless, tongueless mouths of giant clams, opened.

They moved through the green.

She stooped and sought among the shells. When she stood again, she held a huge, eggshell-thin trumpet of pale blue, whorled at the one end into a concavity which might have been a giant's thumbprint, and corkscrewing

112

back to a hooked tail through labyrinths of spaghetti-fine pipette.

"That's it," she said. "The original shell of Daedalus."

"Shell of Daedalus?"

"Know you not the story, m'lord, how the greatest of artificers, Daedalus, did go into hiding one time and was sought by King Minos?"

"I faintly recall . . ."

"Throughout the ancient world did he seek him, but to no avail. For Daedalus, with his arts, could near-duplicate the changes of Proteus. But finally one of the king's advisers hit upon a plan to locate him."

"What was that?"

"By means of this shell, this very shell which I hold before you now and present to you this day, my artificer."

Render took her creation into his hands and studied it.

"He sent it about through the various cities of the Aegean," she explained, "and offered a huge reward to the man who could pass through all its chambers and corridors a single strand of thread."

"I seem to remember . . ."

"How it was done, or why? Minos knew that the only man who could find a way to do it would be the greatest of the artificers, and he also knew the pride of that Daedalus—knew that he would essay the impossible, to prove that he could do what other men could not."

"Yes," said Render, as he passed a strand of silk into the opening at its one end and watched it emerge from the other. "Yes, I remember. A tiny slip-knot, tightened about the middle of a crawling insect—an insect which he induced to enter at the one end, knowing that it was used to dark labyrinths, and that its strength far exceeded its size."

". . . And he strung the shell and collected his reward, and was captured by the king."

"Let that be a lesson to all Shapers—Shape wisely, but not too well."

She laughed.

"But of course he escaped later."

"Of course."

They mounted a stairway of coral.

Render drew the thread, placed the shell to his lips, and blew into it.

A single note sounded beneath the seas.

Where the otter is feeding on fish . . .

The lithe torpedo-shape swam by, invading a school of fish, gulping.

They watched it until it had finished and returned to the surface.

They continued to mount the spiny stairway.

Their heads rose above the water, their shoulders, their arms, their hips, until they stood, dry and warm, on the brief beach. They entered the wood that breasted it and walked beside the stream that flowed down to the sea.

Where the black bear is searching for roots and honey, where the beaver pats the mud with his paddle-shaped tail . . .

"Words," she said, touching her ear.

"Yes, but regard the beaver and the bear."

She did so.

The bees hummed madly about the dark marauder, the mud splattered beneath the tail of the rodent.

"Beaver and bear," she said. "Where are we going now?" as he walked forward again.

" '*Over the growing sugar, over the yellow flower'd cotton plant, over the rice in its low moist field,*' " he replied, and strode ahead.

114

"What are you saying?"

"Look about you and see. Regard the plants, their forms and their colors."

They walked on, walked by.

" '*Over the western persimmon,*' " said Render, " '*over the long-leav'd corn, over the delicate blue-flower flax.*' "

She knelt, and studied, sniffed, touched, tasted.

They walked through the fields, and she felt the black earth beneath her toes.

". . . Something I'm trying to remember," she said.

" '*Over the dusky green of the rye,*' " he said, " '*as it ripples and shades in the breeze.*' "

"Wait a minute, Daedalus," she told him. "It's coming to me, slowly. You're granting me a wish I've never wished aloud."

"Come let us climb a mountain," he suggested, "*holding on by low scragged limbs.*"

They did so, leaving the land far beneath them.

"Rocks, and cold the wind. High, this place," she said. "Where are we going?"

"To the top. To the very top."

They climbed for a timeless instant and stood atop the mountain. Then it seemed that hours had passed in the climbing.

"Distance, perspective," he said. "We have passed through all of that which you see beneath you. Look out across the plains and the forest to the sea."

"We have climbed a fictional mountain," she stated, "which I climbed once before, without seeing it."

He nodded, and the ocean caught her attention again, beneath the other-blue sky.

After a time, she turned away, and they started down the opposite side of the mountain. Again, Time twisted and shaped itself about them, and they stood at the foot of the mountain and moved forward.

" '. . . *Walking the worn path in the grass and beat through the leaves of the brush.'* "

"Now I know!" she said, clapping her hands. "Now I know!"

"Then where are we?" asked Render.

She plucked a single blade of grass, held it before him, then chewed it.

"Where?" she said. "Why, *'Where the quail is whistling betwixt the woods and the wheat-lot,'* of course."

A quail whistled then and crossed their path, the line of its young following as though pulled along on a string.

"Always," she said, "have I wondered what it was all about."

They passed along the darkening path, betwixt the woods and the wheat-lot.

". . . So many things," she said, "like a Sears and Roebuck catalog of the senses. Feed me another line."

"Where the bat flies in the Seventh-month eve,' " said Render, raising his hand.

She ducked her head, before its swoop, and the dark form vanished within the wood.

" *'Where the great gold-bug drops through the dark,'* " she replied.

. . .And it glittered like a 24-karat meteorite and fell to the path at his feet. It lay there for a moment like a sun-colored scarab, then crawled off through the grasses at the side of the trail.

"You remember now," he said.

"I remember now," she told him.

The Seventh-month eve was cool, and pale stars began in the heavens. He pointed out constellations as they walked. A half-moon tipped above the rim of the world, and another bat crossed it. An owl hooted in the distance. Cricket-talk emerged from the undergrowth. A persistent end-of-day glow still filled the world.

"We have come far," she said.

"How far?" he asked.

"To '*where the brook puts out of the roots of the old tree and flows to the meadow,*'" she stated.

"Aye," he said, and he put forth his hand and leaned against the giant tree they had come upon. Rushing forth from among its roots was the spring which fed the stream they had followed earlier. It sounded, like a chain of small bells echoing off into the distance, as it sprang into the air and fell again upon itself and flowed away from them. It wound among the trees, digging into the ground, curling and cutting its way to the sea.

She waded out into the water. It arced over, it foamed about her. It rained down upon her and ran along her back and neck and breasts and arms and legs, returning.

"Come on in, the magic brook is fine," she said.

But Render shook his head and waited.

She emerged, shook herself, was dry.

"Ice and rainbows," she remarked.

"Yes," said Render, "and I forgot much of what comes next."

"So do I, but I remember that a little later on '*the mocking-bird sounds his delicious gurgles, cackles, screams, weeps.*'"

And Render winced as he listened to the mocking-bird.

"That was not my mocking-bird," he stated.

She laughed.

"What difference? His turn was coming up soon, anyhow."

He shook his head and turned away. She was back at his side again.

"I'm sorry. I'll be more careful."

"Very good."

He walked on across the country.

"I forget the next part."

"So do I."

They left the stream far behind them.

They walked through the bending grass, across flat, borderless plains; and all but the peak of the sun's crown vanished over the horizon.

Where sun-down shadows lengthen over the limitless and lonesome prairie . . .

"Did you say something?" she asked.

"No. But I remember again. This is the place '*where herds of buffalo make a crawling spread of the square miles far and near.*'"

A dark mass off to their left gradually took on a more distinct form, and as they watched they could make out the shapes of the great bison of the American plains. Apart from rodeos, cattle shows, and the backs of old nickels, the beasts stood now, individual and dark and smelling of the earth, slow, and huge, and hairy, all together they stood, horned heads lowered, great backs swaying, the sign of Taurus, the inexorable fecundity of spring, fading with the twilight into the passed and the past—*where the humming-bird shimmers,* perhaps.

They crossed the great plain, and the moon was now above them. They came at last to the opposite end of the land, where there were high lakes and another brook, ponds, and another sea. They passed emptied farms and gardens and made their way along the path of the waters.

"'*Where the neck of the long-lived swan is curving*

and winding,'" she said, seeing her first swan in the moonlight drift over the lake.

" *'Where the laughing gull scoots by the shore,'"* he answered, " *'where she laughs her near-human laugh.'"*

And across the night there was laughter, but it was like that of neither laughing gull nor human, for Render had never heard a laughing gull. The chuckling sounds he had shaped from raw emotion chilled the evening around him.

He made the evening come warm again. He lightened the darkness, tinted it with silver. The laughter dwindled and died. A gull-shape departed in the direction of the ocean, dark and silver, dark and silver, turning.

"That," he announced, "is about all for this time."

"But there is more, so much more," she said. "You carry menus about in your head. Don't you remember more of this thing? I remember something about the band-necked partridges roosting in a ring with their heads out, and the yellow-crowned heron feeding upon crabs at the edge of the marsh at night, and the katydid on a walnut tree above a well, and . . ."

"It is rich, it is very rich," said Render. "Too rich, perhaps."

They passed through groves of lemons and oranges, under fir trees, and the places where the heron fed, and the katydid sang on the walnut tree above the well, and the partridges slept in a ring on the ground, heads out.

"Next time, will you name me all the animals?" she asked.

"Yes."

She turned up a little path to a farmhouse, opened the front door, and entered. Render followed her, smiling.

Blackness.

Solid, total—black as only the black of absolute emptiness can be.

There was nothing at all inside the farmhouse.

"What is the matter?" she asked him, from somewhere.

"Unauthorized excursion into the scenery," said Render. "I was about to ring down the curtain and you decided the show should continue. Therefore, I kept myself from providing you with any additional props this time."

"I can't always control it," she said. "I'm sorry. Let us go back now. I've mastered the impulse."

"No, let's go ahead," said Render. "Lights!"

They stood on a high hilltop, and the bats that flitted past the partial moon were metaliic. The evening was chill and a harsh croaking sound arose from a junkpile. The trees were metal posts with the limbs riveted into place. The grass was green plastic underfoot. A gigantic, empty highway swept past the foot of the hill.

"Where—are we?" she asked.

"You've had your *Song of Myself*," he said. "with all the extra narcissism you could stuff in. Nothing wrong with that in this place—up to a point. But you've pushed it a little too far. Now I feel certain balancing has become necessary. I can't afford to play games each session."

"What are you going to do?"

"The *Song of 'Not Me?'* " he stated, clapping his hands. "Let us walk."

. . . *Where the Dust Bowl cries for water,* said a voice, somewhere—and they walked, coughing.

. . . *Where the waste-polluted river knows no living thing,* said the voice, *and the scum is the color of rust.*

They walked beside the stinking river, and she held her nose but it did not stop the smelling.

. . . *Where the forest is laid to waste and the landscape is Limbo.*

They walked among the stumps, stepping on shredded branches; and the dry leaves crackled underfoot. Overhead, the face of the leering moon was scarred, and it hung by a thin strand from the black ceiling.

They walked like giants among wooden plateaus. The earth was cracked beneath the leaves.

. . . Where the curreted land bleeds into the emptied gouge of the strip-mine.

Abandoned machinery lay about them. Mounds of earth and rocks lay bald beneath the night. The great gaps in the ground were filled with a blood-like excrescence.

. . . Sing, Aluminum Muse, who in the beginning taught that shepherd how the museum and the process rose out of Chaos, or if death delight thee more, behold the greatest Graveyard!

They were back atop the hill overlooking the junkheap. It was filled with tractors and bulldozers and steamshovels, with cranes and diggers and trucks. It was piled high with twisted metal, rusted metal, broken metal. Frames and plates and springs and beams lay about, and the blades and shovels and drills were all smashed. It was the Boot Hill of the tool, the Potter's Field of the machine.

"What . . . ?" she said.

"Scrap," said he. "This is the part Walt didn't sing about—the things that step on his blades of grass, the things that tear them up by the roots."

They made their way through the place of dead machinery.

"Haunted, too," he added, "in a way.

"This machine bulldozed an Indian burial mound, and this one cut down the oldest tree on the continent. This one dug a channel which diverted a river which turned a green valley into a wasteland. This one broke in the walls of our ancestors' homes, and this one hoisted the beams up the monstrous towers which replaced them—"

"You're being very unfair," she said.

"Of course," said Render. "You should always try for a large point if you want to make a small one. Remember, I took you where the panther walks to and fro on the limb overhead, and where the rattlesnake suns his flabby length on a rock, and where the alligator in his tough pimples sleeps by the bayou. Do you recall what I said when you asked, 'Why *these* things?' "

"You said, 'More than the idyllic you must know.' "

"Right, and since you were once again so eager to take over, I decided that a little more pain and a little less pleasure might strengthen my position. You've already got whatever goes wrong. I catch it."

"Yes," she said, "I know. But this picture of mechanism paving the road to hell . . . Black or white, really? Which is it?"

"Gray," he told her. "Come a little further."

They rounded a heap of cans and bottles and bedsprings. He stooped beneath a jutting piece of metal and pulled open a hatch.

"Behold hidden in the belly of this great tank truck against the ages of ages!"

Its fantastic glow filled the dark cavity with a soft green light, spreading from where it blazed within a tool box he had flung open.

"Oh . . ."

"The Holy Grail," he announced. "It is enantiadromia, my dear. The circle runs back upon itself. When it passes its beginning, the spiral commences. How can I judge? The Grail may be hidden within a machine. I don't know. Things twist as time goes on. Friends become enemies, evils become benefits. But I'll hold back time long enough to tell you a quick tale, since you regaled me with that of the Greek, Daedalus. It was told me by a patient named Rothman, a student of the Cabala. This Grail you see before you, symbol of light and purity and holiness and heavenly majesty—what is its origin?"

"None is given," she said.

"Ah, but there is a tradition, a legend that Rothman knew: The Grail was handed down by Melchisadek, High Priest of Israel, and destined to reach the hands of the Messiah. But where did Melchisadek get it? He carved it from a gigantic emerald he had found in the wilderness, an emerald which had fallen from the crown of Shmael, Angel of Darkness, as he was cast down from On High. There is your Grail, from light to darkness to light to darkness to who knows? What is the point of it all? Enantiadromia, my dear.—Good-bye, Grail."

He closed the lid and all was darkness.

Then, as he walked on through Winchester Cathedral, flat ceilings everywhere, a statue beheaded (said the guide) by Cromwell, off to his right, he recalled the following session. He remembered his almost-unwilling Adam-attitude as he had named all the animals passing before them, led, of course, by the *one* she wanted to see, colored fearsome by his own unease. He had felt pleasantly bucolic after boning up on an old Botany text and then proceeding to Shape and name the flowers of the field.

So far they had stayed out of the cities, far away from the machines. Her emotions were still too powerful at the sight of the simple, carefully introduced objects to risk plunging her into so complicated and chaotic a wilderness yet; he would built her city slowly.

Something passed rapidly, high above the cathedral, uttering a sonic boom. Render took Jill's hand in his for a moment and smiled as she looked up at him. Knowing she verged upon beauty, Jill normally took great pains to achieve it. But today her hair was simply drawn back and knotted behind her head, and her lips and her eyes were pale; and her exposed ears were tiny and white and somewhat pointed.

"Observe the scalloped capitals," he whispered. "In their primitive fluting they anticipated what was later to become a common motif."

"Faugh!" said she.

"Shh!" said a sunburnt little woman nearby, whose face seemed to crack and fall back together again as she pursed and unpursed her lips.

Later, as they strolled back toward their hotel, Render said, "Okay on Winchester?"

"Okay on Winchester."

"Happy?"

"Happy."

"Good; then we can leave this afternoon."

"All right."

"For Switzerland . . ."

She stopped and toyed with a button on his coat.

"Couldn't we just spend a day or two looking at some old chateaux first? After all, they're just across the Channel, and you could be sampling all the local wines while I looked . . ."

"Okay," he said.

She looked up—a trifle surprised.

"What? No argument?" She smiled. "Where is your fighting spirit?—to let me push you around like this?"

She took his arm then and they walked on as he said, "Yesterday, while we were galloping about in the innards of that old castle, I heard a weak moan, and then a voice cried out, 'For the love of God, Montresor!' I think it was my fighting spirit, because I'm certain it was my voice. I've given up der geist der stets verneint. Pax vobiscum! Let us be gone to France. Alors!"

"Dear Rendy, it'll only be another day or two . . ."

"Amen," he said, "though my skis that were waxed are already waning."

So they did that, and on the morn of the third day, when she spoke to him of castles in Spain, he reflected aloud that while psychologists drink and only grow angry, psychiatrists have been known to drink, grow angry, and break things. Construing this as a veiled threat aimed at the Wedgewoods she had collected, she acquiesced to his desire to skiing.

Free! Render almost screamed it.

His heart was pounding inside his head. He leaned hard. He cut to the left. The wind strapped at his face; a shower of ice crystals, like bullets of emery, fired by him, scraped against his cheek.

He was moving. Aye—the world had ended at Weiss-flujoch, and Dorftali led down and away from this portal.

His feet were two gleaming rivers which raced across the stark, curving plains; they could not be frozen in their course. Downward. He flowed. Away from all the rooms of the world. Away from the stifling lack of intensity, from the day's hundred spoon-fed welfares, from the killing pace of the forced amusements that hacked at the Hydra, leisure; away.

And as he fled down the run he felt a strong desire to look back over his shoulder, as though to see whether the world he had left behind and above had set one fearsome embodiment of itself, like a shadow, to trail along after him, hunt him down, and to drag him back to a warm and well-lit coffin in the sky, there to be laid to rest with a spike of aluminum driven through his will and a garland of alternating currents smothering his spirit.

"I hate you," he breathed between clenched teeth, and the wind carried the words back; and he laughed then, for he always analyzed his emotions, as a matter of reflex; and he added. "Exit Orestes, mad, pursued by the Furies . . ."

After a time the slope leveled out and he reached the bottom of the run and had to stop.

He smoked one cigarette then and rode back up to the top so that he could come down it again for non-therapeutic reasons.

That night he sat before a fire in the big lodge, feeling its warmth soaking into his tired muscles. Jill massaged his shoulders as he played Rorschach with the flames, and he came upon a blazing goblet which was snatched away from him in the same instant by the sound of his name being spoken somewhere across the Hall of the Nine Hearths.

"Charles Render!" said the voice (only it sounded more like "Sharlz Runder"), and his head instantly jerked in that direction but his eyes danced with too many afterimages for him to isolate the source of the calling.

"Maurice?" he queried after a moment, "Bartelmetz?"

"Aye," came the reply, and then Render saw the familiar grizzled visage, set neckless and balding above the red and blue shag sweater that was stretched mercilessly about the wine-keg rotundity of the man who now picked his way in their direction, deftly avoiding the strewn crutches and the stacked skis and the people who, like Jill and Render, disdain sitting in chairs.

"You've put on more weight," Render observed. "That's unhealthy."

"Nonsense, it's all muscle. How have you been and what are you up to these days?" He looked down at Jill and she smiled back at him.

"This is Miss DeVille," said Render.

"Jill," she acknowledged.

He bowed slightly, finally releasing Render's aching hand.

". . . And this is Professor Maurice Bartelmetz of Vienna," finished Render, "a benighted disciple of all forms of dialectical pessimism, and a very distinguished pioneer in neuroparticipation—although you'd never guess it to look at him. I had the good fortune to be his pupil for over a year."

Bartelmetz nodded and agreed with him, taking in the Schnapsflasche Render brought forth from a small plastic bag, and accepting the collapsible cup which he filled to the brim.

"Ah, you are a good doctor still," he sighed. "You have diagnosed the case in an instant and you make the proper prescription. Nozdrovia!"

"Seven years in a gulp," Render acknowledged, refilling their glasses.

"Then we shall make time more malleable by sipping it."

They seated themselves on the floor, and the fire roared up through the great brick chimney as the logs burnt themselves back to branches, to twigs, to thin sticks, ring by yearly ring.

Render replenished the fire.

"I read your last book," said Bartelmetz finally, casually, "about four years ago."

Render reckoned that to be correct.

"Are you doing any research work these days?"

Render poked lazily at the fire.

"Yes," he answered, "sort of."

He glanced at Jill, who was dozing with her cheek against the arm of the huge leather chair that held his emergency bag, the planes of her face all crimson and flickering shadow.

"I've hit upon a rather unusual subject and started with a piece of jobbery I eventually intend to write about."

"Unusual? In what way?"

"Blind from birth, for one thing."

"You're using the ONT&R?"

"Yes. She's going to be a Shaper."

"Verfluchter!—Are you aware of the possible repercussions?"

"Of course."

"You've heard of unlucky Pierre?"

"No."

"Good, then it was successfully hushed. Pierre was a philosophy student at the University of Paris, and he was doing a dissertation on the evolution of consciousness. This past summer he decided it would be necessary for him to explore the mind of an ape, for purposes of comparing a moins-nausee mind with his own, I suppose. At any rate, he obtained illegal access to an ONT&R and to the mind of our hairy cousin. It was never ascertained how far along he got in exposing the animal to the stimuli-bank, but it is to be assumed that such items as would not be immediately trans-subjective between man and ape—traffic sounds und so weiter—were what frightened the creature. Pierre is still residing in a padded cell, and all his responses are those of a frightened ape.

"So, while he did not complete his own dissertation," he finished, "he may provide significant material for some-one else's."

Render shook his head.

"Quite a story," he said softly, "but I have nothing that dramatic to contend with. I've found an exceedingly stable individual—a psychiatrist, in fact—one who's already spent time in ordinary analysis. She wants to go into neuroparticipation—but the fear of a sight-trauma was what was keeping her out. I've been gradually exposing her to a full range of visual phenomena. When I've finished she should be completely accommodated to sight, so that she can give her full attention to therapy and not be blinded by vision, so to speak. We've already had four sessions."

"And?"

". . . And it's working fine."

"You are certain about it?"

"Yes, as certain as anyone can be in these matters."

"Mm-hm," said Bartelmetz. "Tell me, do you find her excessively strong-willed? By that I mean, say, perhaps an obsessive-compulsive pattern concerning anything to which she's been introduced so far?"

"No."

"Has she ever succeeded in taking over control of the fantasy?"

"No!"

"You lie," he said simply.

Render found a cigarette. After lighting it, he smiled.

"Old father, old artificer," he conceded, "age has not withered your perceptiveness. I may trick me, but never you.—Yes, as a matter of fact, she *is* very difficult to keep under control. She is not satisfied just to see. She wants to Shape things for herself already. It's quite understandable—both to her and to me—but conscious apprehension and emotional acceptance never do seem to get together on things. She has become dominant on several occasions, but I've succeeded in resuming control almost immediately. After all, I *am* master of the bank."

"Hm," mused Bartelmetz. "Are you familiar with a Buddhist text—*Shankara's Catechism?*"

"I'm afraid not."

"Then I lecture you on it now. It posits—obviously not for therapeutic purposes—a true ego and a false ego. The true ego is that part of man which is immortal and shall proceed on to nirvana: the soul, if you like. Very good. Well, the false ego, on the other hand, is the normal mind, bound round with the illusions—the consciousness of you and I and everyone we have ever known professionally. Good?—Good. Now, the stuff this false ego is made up of, they call skandhas. These include the feelings, the perceptions, the aptitudes, consciousness itself, and even the physical form. Very unscientific. Yes. Now they are not the same thing as neuroses, or one of Mister Ibsen's life-lies, or an hallucination—no, even though they are all wrong, being parts of a false thing to begin with.

"Each of the five skandhas is a part of the eccentricity that we call identity—then on top come the neuroses and all the other messes which follow after and keep us in business. Okay?—Okay. I give you this lecture because I need a dramatic term for what I will say, because I wish to say something dramatic. View the skandhas as lying at the bottom of the pond; the neuroses, they are ripples on the top of the water; the 'true ego,' if there is one, is buried deep beneath the sand at the bottom. So. The ripples fill up the—the—zwischenwelt—between the object and the subject. The skandhas are a part of the subject, basic, unique, the stuff of his being.—So far, you are with me?"

"With many reservations."

"Good. Now I have defined my term somewhat, I will use it. You are fooling around with skandhas, not simple neuroses. You are attempting to adjust this woman's over-all conception of herself and of the world. You are using the ONT&R to do it. It is the same thing as fooling with a psychotic, or an ape. All may seem to go well, but—at any moment, it is possible you may do something, show her some sight, or some way of seeing which will break in upon her selfhood, break a skandha—and pouf!—it will be like breaking through the bottom of the pond. A whirlpool will result, pulling you—where? I do not want you for a patient, young man, young artificer, so I counsel you not to proceed with this experiment. The ONT&R should not be used in such a manner."

Render flipped his cigarette into the fire and counted on his fingers:

"One," he said, "you are making a mystical mountain out of a pebble. All I am doing is adjusting her consciousness to accept an additional area of perception. Much of it is simple transference work from the other senses.—Two, her emotions were quite intense initially because it *did* involve a trauma—but we've passed that stage already. Now it is only a novelty to her. Soon it will be a commonplace.—Three, Eileen is a psychiatrist herself; she is educated in these matters and deeply aware of the delicate nature of what we are doing.—Four, her sense of identity and her desires, or her skandhas, or whatever you want to call them, are as firm as the Rock of Gibraltar. Do you realize the intense application required for a blind person to obtain the education she has obtained? It took a will of ten-point steel and the emotional control of an ascetic as well—"

"—And if something that strong should break, in a

timeless moment of anxiety"—Bartelmetz smiled sadly—
"may the shades of Sigmund Freud and Karl Jung walk
by your side in the valley of darkness.

"—And five," he added suddenly, staring into Render's
eyes. "Five"—he ticked it off on one finger—"is she
pretty?"

Render looked back into the fire.

"Very clever," sighed Bartelmetz. "I cannot tell
whether you are blushing or not, with the rosy glow of
the flames upon your face. I fear that you are, though,
which would mean that you are aware that you yourself
could be the source of the inciting stimulus. I shall burn a
candle tonight before a portrait of Adler and pray that he
gives you the strength to complete successfully in your
duel with your patient."

Render looked at Jill, who was still sleeping. He
reached out and brushed a lock of her hair back into
place.

"Still," said Bartelmetz, "if you do proceed and all
goes well, I shall look forward with great interest to the
reading of your work. Did I ever tell you that I have
treated several Buddhists and never found a 'true ego'?"

Both men laughed.

Like me but not like me, that one on a leash, smelling
of fear, small, gray and unseeing. *Rrowl* and he'll choke
on his collar. His head is empty as the oven till She
pushes the button and it makes dinner. Make talk and
they never understand, but they are like me. One day I
will kill one—why? . . . Turn here.

"Three steps. Up. Glass doors. Handle to right."

Why? Ahead, drop-shaft. Gardens under, down. Smells
nice, there. Grass, wet dirt, trees and clean air. I see.
Birds are recorded, though. I see all. I.

"Dropshaft. Four steps."

Down. Yes. Want to make loud noises in throat, feel silly. Clean, smooth, many of trees. God . . . She likes sitting on bench, chewing leaves smelling smooth air. Can't see them like me. Maybe now, some . . . ? No.

Can't Bad Sigmund me on grass, trees, here. Must hold it. Pity. Best place . . .

"Watch for steps."

Ahead. To right, to left, to right, to left, trees and grass now. Sigmund sees. Walking . . . Doctor with machine gives her his eyes. *Rrowl* and he will not choke. No fear-smell.

Dig deep hole in ground, bury eyes. God is blind. Sigmund to see. Her eyes now filled, and he is afraid of teeth. Will make her to see and take her high up in the sky to see, away. Leave me here, leave Sigmund with none to see, alone. I will dig a deep hole in the ground . . .

It was after ten in the morning when Jill awoke. She did not have to turn her head to know that Render was already gone. He never slept late. She rubbed her eyes, stretched, turned onto her side and raised herself on her elbows. She squinted at the clock on the bedside table, simultaneously reaching for a cigarette and her lighter.

As she inhaled, she realized there was no ashtray. Doubtless Render had moved it to the dresser because he did not approve of smoking in bed. With a sigh that ended in a snort she slid out of bed and drew on her wrap before the ash grew too long.

She hated getting up, but once she did she would permit the day to begin and continue on without lapse through its orderly progression of events.

"Damn him." She smiled. She had wanted her breakfast in bed, but it was too late now.

Between thoughts as to what she would wear, she observed an alien pair of skis standing in the corner. A sheet of paper was impaled on one. She approached it.

"Join me?" asked the scrawl.

She shook her head in an emphatic negative and felt somewhat sad. She had been on skis twice in her life and she was afraid of them. She felt that she should really try again, after his being a reasonably good sport about the chateaux, but she could not even bear the memory of the unseemly downward rushing—which, on two occasions, had promptly deposited her in a snowbank—without wincing and feeling once again the vertigo that had seized her during the attempts.

So she showered and dressed and went downstairs for breakfast.

All nine fires were already roaring as she passed the big hall and looked inside. Some red-faced skiers were holding their hands up before the blaze of the central hearth. It was not crowded though. The racks held only a few pairs of dripping boots, bright caps hung on pegs, moist skis stood upright in their place beside the door. A few people were seated in the chairs set further back toward the center of the hall, reading papers, smoking, or talking quietly. She saw no one she knew, so she moved on toward the dining room.

As she passed the registration deck the old man who worked there called out her name. She approached him and smiled.

"Letter," he explained, turning to a rack. "Here it is," he announced, handing it to her. "Looks important."

It had been forwarded three times, she noted. It was a

bulky brown envelope, and the return address was that of her attorney.

"Thank you."

She moved off to a seat beside the big window that looked out upon a snow garden, a skating rink, and a distant winding trail dotted with figures carrying skis over their shoulders. She squinted against the brightness as she tore open the envelope.

Yes, it was final. Her attorney's note was accompanied by a copy of the divorce decree. She had only recently decided to end her legal relationship to Mister Fotlock, whose name she had stopped using five years earlier, when they had separated. Now that she had the thing she wasn't sure exactly what she was going to do with it. It would be a hell of a surprise for dear Rendy, though, she decided. She would have to find a reasonably innocent way of getting the information to him. She withdrew her compact and practiced a "Well?" expression. Well, there would be time for that later, she mused. Not too much later, though . . . Her thirtieth birthday, like a huge black cloud, filled an April but four months distant. Well . . . She touched her quizzical lips with color, dusted more powder over her mole, and locked the expression within her compact for future use.

In the dining room she saw Dr. Bartelmetz, seated before an enormous mound of scrambled eggs, great chains of dark sausages, several heaps of yellow toast, and a half-emptied flask of orange juice. A pot of coffee steamed on the warmer at his elbow. He leaned slightly forward as he ate, wielding his fork like a windmill blade.

"Good morning," she said.

He looked up.

"Miss DeVille—Jill . . . Good morning." He nodded at the chair across from him. "Join me, please."

She did so, and when the waiter approached she nodded and said, "I'll have the same thing, only about ninety percent less."

She turned back to Bartelmetz.

"Have you seen Charles today?"

"Alas, I have not"—he gestured, open-handed—"and I wanted to continue our discussion while his mind was still in the early stages of wakefulness and somewhat malleable. Unfortunately"—he took a sip of coffee—"he who sleeps well enters the day somewhere in the middle of the second act."

"Myself, I usually come in around intermission and ask someone for a synopsis," she explained. "So why not continue the discussion with me?—I'm always malleable, and my skandhas are in good shape."

Their eyes met, and he took a bite of toast.

"Aye," he said, at length. "I had guessed as much. Well—good. What do you know of Render's work?"

She adjusted herself in the chair.

"Mm. He being a special specialist in a highly specialized area, I find it difficult to appreciate the few things he does say about it. I'd like to be able to look inside other people's minds sometimes—to see what they're thinking about *me,* of course—but I don't think I could stand staying there very long. Especially"—she gave a mock-shudder—"the mind of somebody with—problems. I'm afraid I'd be too sympathetic or too frightened or something. Then, according to what I've read—pow!—like sympathetic magic, it would be my problems.

"Charles never has problems though," she continued, "at least, none that he speaks to me about. Lately I've been wondering, though. That blind girl and her talking dog seem to be too much for him."

"Talking dog?"

"Yes, her seeing-eye dog is one of those surgical mutants."

"How interesting . . . Have you ever met her?"

"Never."

"So," he mused.

"Sometimes a therapist encounters a patient whose problems are so akin to his own that the sessions become extremely mordant," he noted. "It has always been the case with me when I treat a fellow-psychiatrist. Perhaps Charles sees in this situation a parallel to something which has been troubling him personally. I did not administer his personal analysis. I do not know all the ways of his mind, even though he was a pupil of mine for a long while. He was always self-contained, somewhat reticent; he could be quite authoritative on occasion, however.—What are some of the other things which occupy his attention these days?"

"His son Peter is a constant concern. He's changed the boy's school five times in five years."

Her breakfast arrived. She adjusted her napkin and drew her chair closer to the table.

"—and he has been reading case histories of suicides recently, and talking about them, and talking about them, and talking about them."

"To what end?"

She shrugged and began eating.

"He never mentioned why," she said, looking up again. "Maybe he's writing something . . ."

Bartelmetz finished his eggs and poured more coffee.

"Are you afraid of this patient of his?" he inquired.

"No . . . Yes," she responded, "I am."

"Why?"

"I am afraid of sympathetic magic," she said, flushing slightly.

"Many things could fall under that heading."

"Many indeed," she acknowledged. And, after a moment, "We are united in our concern for his welfare and in agreement as to what represents the threat. So, may I ask a favor?"

"You may."

"Talk to him again," she said. "Persuade him to drop the case."

He folded his napkin.

"I intended to do that after dinner," he stated, "because I believe in the ritualistic value of rescue-motions. They shall be made."

Dear Father-Image,

Yes, the school is fine, my ankle is getting that way, and my classmates are a congenial lot. No, I am not short on cash, undernourished, or having difficulty fitting into the new curriculum. Okay?

The building I will not describe, as you have already seen the macabre thing. The grounds I cannot describe, as they are presently residing beneath cold white sheets. Brr! I trust yourself to be enjoying the arts wint'rish. I do not share your enthusiasm for summer's opposite, except within picture frames or as an emblem on ice cream bars.

The ankle inhibits my mobility and my roommate has gone home for the weekend—both of which are really blessings (saith Pangloss), for I now have the opportunity to catch up on some reading. I will do so forthwith.

Prodigially,
Peter

Render reached down to pat the huge head. It accepted the gesture stoically, then turned its gaze up to the Austrian whom Render had asked for a light, as if to say, "Must I endure this indignity?" The man laughed at the expression, snapping shut the engraved lighter on which Render noted the middle initial to be a small "v."

"Thank you," he said, and to the dog: "What is your name?"

"Bismark," it growled.

"You remind me of another of your kind," he told the dog. "One Sigmund, by name, a companion and guide to a blind friend of mine, in America."

"My Bismark is a hunter," said the young man. "There is no quarry that can outthink him, neither the deer nor the big cats."

The dog's ears pricked forward and he stared up at Render with proud, blazing eyes.

"We have hunted in Africa and the northern and southwestern parts of America. Central America, too. He never loses the trail. He never gives up. He is a beautiful brute, and his teeth could have been made in Solingen."

"You are indeed fortunate to have such a hunting companion."

"I hunt," growled the dog. "I follow . . . Sometimes, I have, the kill . . ."

"You would not know of the one called Sigmund then, or the woman he guides—Miss Eileen Shallot?" asked Render.

The man shook his head.

"No, Bismark came to me from Massachusetts, but I was never to the Center personally. I am not acquainted with other mutie handlers."

"I see. Well, thank you for the light. Good afternoon."

"Good afternoon."

"Good, after, noon . . ."

Render strolled on up the narrow street, hands in his pockets. He had excused himself and not said where he was going. This was because he had had no destination in mind. Bartelmetz' second essay at counseling had almost led him to say things he would later regret. It was easier to take a walk than to continue the conversation.

On a sudden impulse he entered a small shop and bought a cuckoo clock which had caught his eye. He felt certain that Bartelmetz would accept the gift in the proper spirit. He smiled and walked on. And what was that letter to Jill which the desk clerk had made a special trip to their table to deliver at dinnertime? he wondered. It had been forwarded three times, and its return address was that of a law firm. Jill had not even opened it, but had smiled, overtipped the old man, and tucked it into her purse. He would have to hint subtly as to its contents. His curiosity so aroused that she would be sure to tell him out of pity.

The icy pillars of the sky suddenly seemed to sway before him as a cold wind leapt down out of the north. Render hunched his shoulders and drew his head further below his collar. Clutching the cuckoo clock, he hurried back up the street.

That night the serpent which holds its tail in its mouth belched, the Fenris Wolf made a pass at the moon, the little clock said "cuckoo" and tomorrow came on like Manolete's last bull, shaking the gate of horn with the bellowed promise to tread a river of lions to sand.

Render promised himself he would lay off the gooey fondue.

Later, much later, when they skipped through the skies in a kite-shaped cruiser, Render looked down upon the darkened Earth dreaming its cities full of stars, looked up at the sky where they were all reflected, looked about him at the tape-screens watching all the people who blinked into them, and at the coffee, tea, and mixed drink dispensers who sent their fluids forth to explore the insides of the people they required to push their buttons, then looked across at Jill, whom the old buildings had compelled to walk among their walls—because he knew she felt he should be looking at her then—felt his seat's demand that he convert it into a couch, did so, and slept.

V

HER OFFICE was full of flowers, and she liked exotic perfumes. Sometimes she burned incense.

She liked soaking in overheated pools, walking through falling snow, listening to too much music, played perhaps too loudly, drinking five or six varieties of liqueurs (usually reeking of anise, sometimes touched with wormwood) every evening. Her hands were soft and lightly freckled. Her fingers were long and tapered. She wore no rings.

Her fingers traced and retraced the floral swellings on the side of her chair as she spoke into the recording unit.

". . . Patient's chief complaints on admission were nervousness, insomnia, stomach pains and a period of depression. Patient has had a record of previous admissions for short periods of time. He had been in this hospital in 1995 for a manic depressive psychosis, depressed type, and he returned here again, 2-3-96. He was in another hospital, 9-20-97. Physical examination revealed a BP of 170/100. He was normally developed and well-nourished on the date of examination 12-11-98. On this date patient complained of chronic backache, and there was noted some moderate symptoms of alcohol withdrawal. Physical examination further revealed no pathology except that the patient's tendon reflexes were exaggerated but equal. These symptoms were the result of alcohol withdrawal. Upon admission he was shown to be not psychotic, neither delusional nor hallucinated. He was well-oriented as to place, time and person. His psychological condition was evaluated and he was found to be somewhat grandiose and expansive and more than a little hostile. He was considered a potential troublemaker. Because of his experience as a cook, he was assigned to work in the kitchen. His general condition then showed definite improvement. He is less tense and is cooperative. Diagnosis: Manic depressive reaction (external precipitating stress unknown.) The degree of psychiatric impairment is mild. He is considered competent. To be continued on therapy and hospitalization."

She turned off the recorder then and laughed. The sound frightened her. Laughter is a social phenomenon and she was alone. She played back the recording then, chewing on the corner of her handkerchief while the soft, clipped words were returned to her. She ceased to hear them after the first dozen or so.

When the recorder stopped talking she turned it off. She was alone. She was very alone. She was so damned alone that the little pool of brightness which occurred when she stroked her forehead and faced the window—that little pool of brightness suddenly became the most important thing in the world. She wanted it to be an ocean of light. Or else she wanted to grow so small herself that the effect would be the same: she wanted to drown in it.

It had been three weeks, yesterday . . .

Too long, she decided, *I should have waited. No! Impossible! But what if he goes as Riscomb went? No! He won't. He would not. Nothing can hurt him. Never. He is all strength and armor. But—but we should have waited till next month to start. Three weeks . . . Sight withdrawal—that's what it is. Are the memories fading? Are*

*they weaker? (What does a tree look like? Or a cloud?—
I can't remember! What is red? What is green? God! It's
hysteria! I'm watching and I can't stop it!—take a pill!
A pill!)*

Her shoulders began to shake. She did not take a pill,
though, but bit down harder on the handkerchief until
her sharp teeth tore through its fabric.

"Beware," she recited a personal beatitude, "those who
hunger and thirst after justice, for we *will* be satisfied.

"And beware the meek," she continued, "for we shall
attempt to inherit the Earth.

"And beware . . ."

There was a brief buzz from the phone-box. She put
away her handkerchief, composed her face, turned the
unit on.

"Hello . . . ?"

"Eileen, I'm back. How've you been?"

"Good, quite well in fact. How was your vacation?"

"Oh, I can't complain. I had it coming for a long time.
I guess I deserve it. Listen, I brought some things back
to show you—like Winchester Cathedral. You want to
come in this week? I can make it any evening."

*Tonight. No. I want it too badly. It will set me back
if he sees . . .*

"How about tomorrow night?" she asked. "Or the one
after?"

"Tomorrow will be fine," he said. "Meet you at the
P & S, around seven?"

"Yes, that would be pleasant. Same table?"

"Why not?—I'll reserve it."

"All right. I'll see you then."

"Good-bye."

The connection was broken.

Suddenly, then, at that moment, colors swirled again

through her head; and she saw trees—oaks and pines, poplars and sycamores—great, and green and brown, and iron-colored; and she saw wads of fleecy clouds, dipped in paintpots, swabbing a pastel sky; and a burning sun, and a small willow tree, and a lake of deep, almost violet, blue. She folded her torn handkerchief and put it away.

She pushed a button beside her desk and music filled the office: Scriabin. Then she pushed another button and replayed the tape she had dictated, half-listening to each.

Pierre sniffed suspiciously at the food. The attendant moved away from the tray and stepped out into the hall, locking the door behind him. The enormous salad waited on the floor. Pierre approached cautiously, snatched a handful of lettuce, gulped it.

He was afraid.

If only the steel would stop crashing, and crashing against steel, somewhere in that dark night. . . . If only . . .

Sigmund rose to his feet, yawned, stretched. His hind legs trailed out behind him for a moment, then he snapped to attention and shook himself. She would be coming home soon. Wagging his tail slowly, he glanced up at the human-level clock with the raised numerals, verified his feelings, then crossed the apartment to the teevee. He rose onto his hind legs, rested one paw against the table and used the other to turn on the set.

It was nearly time for the weather report and the roads would be icy.

"I have driven through countrywide graveyards," wrote Render, "vast forests of stone that spread further every day.

"Why does man so zealously guard his dead? Is it because this is the monumentally democratic way of immortalization, the ultimate affirmation of the power to hurt—that is to say, life—and the desire that it continue on forever? Unamuno has suggested that this is the case. If it is, then a greater percentage of the population actively sought immortality last year than ever before in history . . ."

Tch-tchg, tchga-tchg!
"Do you think they're really people?"
"Naw, they're too good."

The evening was starglint and soda over ice. Render wound the S-7 into the cold sub-subcellar, found his parking place, nosed into it.

There was a damp chill that emerged from the concrete to gnaw like rats' teeth at their flesh. Render guided her toward the left, their breath preceding them in dissolving clouds.

"A bit of a chill in the air," he noted.

She nodded, biting her lip.

Inside the lift, he sighed, unwound his scarf, lit a cigarette.

"Give me one, please," she requested, smelling the tobacco.

He did.

They rose slowly, and Render leaned against the wall, puffing a mixture of smoke and crystalized moisture.

"I met another mutie shep," he recalled, "in Switzerland. Big as Sigmund. A hunter though, and as Prussian as they come." He grinned.

"Sigmund likes to hunt, too," she observed. "Twice every year we go up to the North Woods and I turn him loose. He's gone for days at a time, and he's always quite happy when he returns. Never says what he's done, but he's never hungry. Back when I got him I guessed that he would need vacations from humanity to stay stable. I think I was right."

The lift stopped, the door opened, and they walked out into the hall, Render guiding her again.

Inside his office, he poked at the thermostat and warm air sighed through the room. He hung their coats in the inner office and brought the great egg out from its nest behind the wall. He connected it to an outlet and moved to convert his desk into a control panel.

"How long do you think it will take?" she asked, running her fingertips over the smooth, cold curves of the egg. "The whole thing, I mean. The entire adaptation to seeing."

He wondered.

"I have no idea," he said, "no idea whatsoever, yet. We got off to a good start, but there's still a lot of work to be done. I think I'll be able to make a good guess in another three months."

She nodded wistfully, moved to his desk, explored the controls with fingerstrokes like ten feathers.

"Careful you don't push any of those."

"I won't. How long do you think it will take me to learn to operate one?"

"Three months to learn it. Six, to actually become proficient enough to use it on anyone; and an additional six under close supervision before you can be trusted on your own. About a year altogether."

"Uh-huh." She chose a chair.

Render touched the seasons to life, and the phases of day and night, the breath of the country, the city, the elements that raced naked through the skies, and all the dozens of dancing cues he used to build worlds. He smashed the clock of time and tasted the seven or so ages of man.

"Okay,"—he turned—"everything is ready."

It came quickly, and with a minimum of suggestion on Render's part. One moment there was grayness. Then a dead-white fog. Then it broke itself apart, as though a quick wind had risen, although he heard nor felt a wind.

He stood beside the willow tree beside the lake, and she stood half-hidden among the branches and the lattices of shadow. The sun was slanting its way into evening.

"We have come back," she said, stepping out, leaves in her hair. "For a time I was afraid it had never happened, but I see it all again, and I remember now."

"Good," he said. "Behold yourself." And she looked into the lake.

"I have not changed," she said. "I haven't changed . . ."

"No."

"But you have," she continued. looking up at him. "You are taller, and there is something different . . ."

"No," he answered.

"I am mistaken," she said quickly, "I don't understand everything I see yet.

"I will though."

"Of course."

"What are we going to do?"

"Watch," he instructed her.

Along a flat, no-colored river of road she just then noticed beyond the trees, came the car. It came from the farthest quarter of the sky, skipping over the mountains, buzzing down the hills, circling through the glades, and splashing them with the colors of its voice—the gray and the silver of synchronized potency—and the lake shivered from its sounds, and the car stopped a hundred feet away, masked by the shrubberies; it waited. It was the S-7.

"Come with me," he said, taking her hand. "We're going for a ride."

They walked among the trees and rounded the final cluster of bushes. She touched the sleek cocoon, its antennae, its tires, its windows—and the windows transpared as she did so. She stared through them at the inside of the car, and she nodded,

"It is your Spinner."

"Yes." He held the door for her. "Get in. We'll return to the club. The time is now. The memories are fresh, and they should be reasonably pleasant, or neutral."

"Pleasant," she said, getting in.

He closed the door, then circled the car and entered. She watched as he punched imaginary coordinates. The car leapt ahead and he kept a steady stream of trees flowing by them. He could feel the rising tension, so he did not vary the scenery. She swiveled her seat and studied the interior of the car.

"Yes," she finally said, "I can perceive what everything is."

She stared out the window again. She looked at the rushing trees. Render stared out and looked upon rushing anxiety patterns. He opaqued the windows.

"Good," she said, "thank you. Suddenly it was too much to see—all of it, moving past like a . . ."

"Of course," said Render, maintaining the sensations of forward motion. "I'd anticipated that. You're getting tougher, though."

After a moment, "Relax,"! he said, "relax now," and somewhere a button was pushed; and she relaxed and they drove on, and on and on, and finally, the car began to slow, and Render said, "Just for one nice, slow glimpse now, look out your window."

She did.

He drew upon every stimulus in the bank which could promote sensations of pleasure and relaxation, and he dropped the city around the car, and the windows became transparent, and she looked out upon the profiles of towers and a block of monolithic apartments, and then she saw three rapid cafeterias, an entertainment palace, a drugstore, a medical center of yellow brick with an aluminum caduceus set above its archways, and a glassed-in high school, now emptied of its pupils, a fifty-pump gas station, another drugstore, and many more cars, parked or roaring by them, and people, people moving in and out of the doorways and walking before the buildings and getting into the cars and getting out of the cars; and it was summer, and the light of late afternoon filtered down upon the colors of the city and the colors of the garments the people wore as they moved along the boulevard, as they loafed upon the terraces, as they crossed the balconies, leaned on balustrades and windowsills, emerged from a corner kiosk, entered one, stood talking to one another; a woman walking a poodle rounded a corner; rockets went to and fro in the high sky.

The world fell apart then and Render caught the pieces.

He maintained an absolute blackness, blanketing every sensation but that of their movement forward.

After a time a dim light occurred, and they were still seated in the Spinner, windows blanked again, and the air as they breathed it became a soothing unguent.

"Lord," she said, "the world is so filled. Did I really see all of that?"

"I wasn't going to do that tonight, but you wanted me to. You seemed ready."

"Yes," she said, and the windows became transparent again. She turned away quickly.

"It's gone," he said. "I only wanted to give you a glimpse."

She looked, and it was dark outside now, and they were crossing over a high bridge. They were moving slowly. There was no other traffic. Below them were the Flats, where an occasional smelter flared like a tiny, drowsing volcano, spitting showers of orange sparks skyward; and there were many stars: they glistened on the breathing water that went beneath the bridge; they silhouetted by pin-prick the skyline that hovered dimly below its surface. The slanting struts of the bridge marched steadily by.

"You have done it," she said, "and I thank you." Then: "Who are you, really?" (He must have wanted her to ask that.)

"I am Render." He laughed. And they wound their way through a dark, now-vacant city, coming at last to their club and entering the great parking dome.

Inside, he scrutinized all her feelings, ready to banish the world at a moment's notice. He did not feel he would have to, though.

They left the car, moved ahead. They passed into the club, which he had decided would not be crowded tonight. They were shown to their table at the foot of the bar in the small room with the suit of armor, and they sat down and ordered the same meal over again.

"No," he said, looking down, "it belongs over there."

The suit of armor appeared once again beside the table, and he was once again inside his gray suit and black tie and silver tie clasp shaped like a treelimb.

They laughed.

"I'm just not the type to wear a tin suit, so I wish you'd stop seeing me that way."

"I'm sorry." She smiled. "I don't know how I did that, or why."

"I do, and I decline the nomination. Also, I caution you once again. You are conscious of the fact that this is all an illusion. I had to do it that way for you to get the full benefit of the thing. For most of my patients though, it is the real item while they are experiencing it. It makes a counter-trauma or a symbolic sequence even more powerful. You are aware of the parameters of the game, however, and whether you want it or not this gives you a different sort of control over it than I normally have to deal with. Please be careful."

"I'm sorry. I didn't mean to."

"I know. Here comes the meal we just had."

"Ugh! It looks dreadful! Did we eat all that stuff?"

"Yes." He chuckled. "That's a knife, that's a fork, that's a spoon. That's roast beef, and those are mashed potatoes, those are peas, that's butter . . ."

"Goodness! I don't feel so well."

". . . And those are the salads, and those are the salad dressings. This is a brook trout—mm! These are French fried potatoes. This is a bottle of wine. Hmm—let's see—Romanee-Conti, since I'm not paying for it—and a bottle of Yquem for the trou—Hey!"

The room was wavering.

He bared the table, he banished the restaurant. They were back in the glade. Through the transparent fabric of the world he watched a hand moving along a panel. Buttons were being pushed. The world grew substantial again. Their emptied table was set beside the lake now, and it was still nighttime and summer, and the tablecloth was very white under the glow of the giant moon that hung overhead.

"That was stupid of me," he said. "Awfully stupid. I should have introduced them one at a time. The actual sight of basic, oral stimuli can be very distressing to a person seeing them for the first time. I got so wrapped up in the Shaping that I forgot the patient, which is just dandy! I apologize."

"I'm okay now. Really I am."

He summoned a cool breeze from the lake.

". . . And that is the moon," he said lamely.

She nodded, and she was wearing a tiny moon in the center of her forehead; it glowed like the one above them, and her hair and dress were all of silver.

The bottle of Romanee-Conti stood on the table, and two glasses.

"Where did that come from?"

She shrugged. He poured out a glassful.

"It may taste kind of flat," he said.

"It doesn't. Here——" She passed it to him.

As he sipped it he realized it had a taste—a *fruite* such as might be quashed from the grapes grown in the Isles of the Blest, a smooth, muscular *charnu,* and a *capiteux* centrifuged from the fumes of a field of burning poppies. With a start, he knew that his hand must be traversing the route of the perceptions, symphonizing the sensual cues of a transference and a counter-transference which had come upon him all unawares, there beside the lake.

"So it does," he noted, "and now it is time we returned."

"So soon? I haven't seen the cathedral yet . . ."

"So soon."

He willed the world to end and it did.

153

"It is cold out there," she said as she dressed, "and dark."

"I know. I'll mix us something to drink while I clear the unit."

"Fine."

He glanced at the tapes and shook his head. He crossed to his bar cabinet.

"It's not exactly Romanee-Conti," he observed, reaching for a bottle.

"So what? I don't mind."

Neither did he, at that moment. So he cleared the unit, they drank their drinks, and he helped her into her coat and they left.

As they rode the lift down to the sub-sub he willed the world to end again, but it didn't.

"There are approximately 1 billion 80 million people in the country at this time, and 560 million private automobiles. If a man occupies two square feet of land and a vehicle approximately 120, then it becomes apparent that while people take up 2 billion 160 million square feet of our country, vehicles occupy 67.2 billion square feet, or approximately 31 times the space of mankind. If, at this moment, half of these vehicles are in operation and containing an average of two passengers, then the ratio is better than 47 to 1 in favor of the cars.

"As soon as the country is made into a single paved plain, and the people either return to the seas from which they came, remove themselves to dwellings beneath the surface of the earth, or emigrate to other planets, then perhaps technological evolution will be permitted to continue along the lines which statistics have laid down for its guidance."

DREAM MASTER

Sybil K. Delphi, Professor Emeritus,
Commencement Address
Broken Rock State Teachers' College.
Shotover, Utah

Dad,

I hobbled from school to taxi and taxi to spaceport, for the local Air Force Exhibit—Outward, it was called. (Okay, I exaggerated the hobble. It got me extra attention though.) The whole bit was aimed at seducing young manhood into a five-year hitch, as I saw it. But it worked. I wanna join up. I wanna go Out there. Think they'll take me when I'm old enuff? I mean take me Out—not some crummy desk job. Think so?

I do.

There was this dam lite colonel ('scuse the French) who saw this kid lurching around and pressing his nose 'gainst the big windowpanes, and he decided to give him the subliminal sell. Great! He pushed me through the gallery and showed me all the pitchers of AF triumphs, from Moonbase to Marsport. He lectured me on the Great Traditions of the Service, and marched me into a flic room where the Corps had good clean fun on tape, wrestling one another in nul-G "where it's all skill and no brawn," and making tinted water sculpture-work in the middle of the air and doing dismounted drill on the skin of a cruiser. Oh joy!

Seriously though, I'd like to be there when they hit the Outer Five—and On Out. Not because of the bogus balonus in the throwaways, and suchlike crud, but because I think someone of sensibility should be along to chronicle the thing in the proper way. You know, raw frontier observer. Francis Parkman. Mary Austin, like that. So I decided I'm going.

*The AF boy with the chicken stuff on his shoulders
wasn't in the least way patronizing, gods be praised. We
stood on the balcony and watched ships lift off and he
told me to go forth and study real hard and I might be
riding them some day. I did not bother to tell him that
I'm hardly intellectually deficient and that I'll have my
B.A. before I'm old enough to do anything with it, even
join his Corps. I just watched the ship lift off and said,
"Ten years from now I'll be looking down, not up."
Then he told me how hard his own training had been, so
I did not ask howcum he got stuck with a lousy dirtside
assignment like this one. Glad I didn't, now I think on
it. He looked more like one of their ads than one of their
real people. Hope I never look like an ad.*

*Thank you for the monies and the warm sox and
Mozart's String Quintets, which I'm hearing right now.
I wanna put in my bid for Luna instead of Europe next
summer. Maybe . . . ? Possibly . . . ? Contingently
. . . ? Huh— If I can smash that new test you're de-
signing for me . . . ? Anyhow, please think about it.*

Your son,
Pete

"Hello. *State Psychiatric Institute.*"

"I'd like to make an appointment for an examination."

"Just a moment. I'll connect you with the Appointment Desk."

"Hello. Appointment Desk."

"I'd like to make an appointment for an examination."

"Just a moment . . . What sort of examination."

"I want to see Dr. Shallot, Eileen Shallot. As soon as
possible."

"Just a moment. I'll have to check her schedule. . . .
Could you make it at two o'clock next Tuesday?"

"That would be just fine."

"What is the name, please?"

"DeVille. Jill DeVille."

"All right, Miss Deville. That's two o'clock, Tuesday."

"Thank you."

*The man walked beside the highway. Cars passed
along the highway. The cars in the high-acceleration lane
blurred by.*

Traffic was light.

It was 10:30 in the morning, and cold.

*The man's fur-lined collar was turned up, his hands
were in his pockets, and he leaned into the wind. Beyond
the fence, the road was clean and dry.*

*The morning sun was buried in clouds. In the dirty
light, the man could see the tree a quarter mile ahead.*

*His pace did not change. His eyes did not leave the
tree. The small stones clicked and crunched beneath his
shoes.*

*When he reached the tree he took off his jacket and
folded it neatly.*

He placed it upon the ground and climbed the tree.

*As he moved out onto the limb which extended over
the fence, he looked to see that no traffic was approach-
ing. Then he seized the branch with both hands, lowered
himself, hung a moment, and dropped onto the highway.*

*It was a hundred yards wide, the eastbound half of
the highway.*

*He glanced west, saw there was still no traffic coming
his way, then began to walk toward the center island. He
knew he would never reach it. At this time of day the*

cars were moving at approximately one hundred-sixty miles an hour in the high-acceleration lane. He walked on.

A car passed behind him. He did not look back. If the windows were opaqued, as was usually the case, then the occupants were unaware he had crossed their path. They would hear of it later and examine the front end of their vehicle for possible sign of such an encounter.

A car passed in front of him. Its windows were clear. A glimpse of two faces, their mouths made into O's, was presented to him, then torn from his sight. His own face remained without expression. His face did not change. Two more cars rushed by, windows darkened. He had crossed perhaps twenty yards of highway.

Twenty-five . . .

Something in the wind, or beneath his feet, told him it was coming. He did not look.

Something in the corner of his eye assured him it was coming. His gait did not alter.

Cecil Green had the windows transpared because he liked it that way. His left hand was inside her blouse and her skirt was piled up on her lap, and his right hand was resting on the lever which would lower the seats. Then she pulled away, making a noise down inside her throat.

His head snapped to the left.

He saw the walking man.

He saw the profile which never turned to face him fully. He saw that the man's gait did not alter.

Then he did not see the man.

There was a slight jar, and the windshield began cleaning itself. Cecil Green raced on.

He opaqued the windows.

"How . . . ?" he asked after she was in his arms again, and sobbing.

"The monitor didn't pick him up . . ."
"He must not have touched the fence . . ."
"He must have been out of his mind!"
"Still, he could have picked an easier way."
It could have been any face . . . Mine?
Frightened, Cecil lowered the seats.

—Hello, kiddies. That's a closeup of a big, fat, tobacco-stained smile you were just rewarded with. So much for humor. This evening we are going to depart from our unusual informal format. We are going to begin with a meticulously contrived dramatic presentation in the latest art-mode:

We are going to Act a Myth.

—It was only after considerable soul-searching and morbid introspection that we decided to act out *this* particular myth for you this night.

—Ptui!

—Yes, I'm chewing tobacco—Red Man, a real good brand—that's a free plug.

—Now, as I jump up and down and spit about the stage, who will be the first to identify my mythic agony? Don't all rush for your phones.—Ptui!

—That's right, ladies and gentlemen and everybody else: I am Tithonus—immortal, decrepit, and turning into a grasshopper.—Ptui!

—Now, for my next number, I'll need more light.

—More light than that.—Ptui!

—Much more light than that . . .

—Blinding light! —Dazzling light!

—Very good. —Ptui!

—Now—into my pilot's jacket, sunshades, silk scarf—there! Where's my whip?

—All right, all set.

—Up you huskies! Mush! Mush! Gee! Haw! Haw! Up! Up! Up! into the air with you, you immortal horses, you! G'wan, now! Get up there!

—More light!

—C'mon, you horses, you! Faster! Higher! Dad and Mom are watching, and that's my girl down there! C'mon! Don't disgrace yourselves at this altitude now! Mush!

—What the devil is *that* coming toward me? It looks like a thunderbooooo—aaaaaah!

—Uh. That was Phaeton, blindspinning in the sun-chariot.

—Next, you've all probably heard the old saying, 'Only a god can make a tree.' Well, this myth is entitled 'Apollo and Daphne.' —Kill those kleigs . . . !

Charles Render was writing the "Necropolis" chapter for *The Missing Link is Man,* which was to be his first book in over four years. Since his return he had set aside every Tuesday and Thursday afternoons to work on it, isolating himself in his office, filling pages with a chaotic longhand.

"There are many varieties of death, as opposed to dying . . ." he was writing, just as the intercom buzzed briefly, then long, then again briefly.

"Yes?" he asked it, pushing down on the switch.

"You have a visitor," and there was a short intake of breath between "a" and "visitor."

He slipped a small aerosol into his side pocket, then rose and crossed the office.

He opened the door and looked out.

"Doctor . . . Help . . ."

Render took three steps, then dropped to one knee.

"What's the matter?"

"Come, she is . . . sick," he growled.

"Sick? How? What's wrong?"

"Don't know. You come."

Render stared into the unhuman eyes.

"What kind of sick?" he insisted.

"Don't know," repeated the dog. "Won't talk. Sits. I
. . . feel, she is sick."

"How did you get here?"

"Drove. Know the co, or, din, ates . . . Left car, out-side."

"I'll call her right now." Render turned.

"No good. Won't answer."

He was right.

Render returned to his inner office for his coat and
med-kit. He glanced out the window and saw where
her car was parked, far below, just inside the entrance
to the marginal, where the monitor had released it into
manual control. If no one assumed that control a car
was automatically parked in neutral. The other vehicles
were passed around it.

So simple even a dog can drive one, he reflected. *Better
get downstairs before a cruiser comes along. It's probably
reported itself stopped there already. Maybe not, though.
Might still have a few minutes grace.*

He glanced at the huge clock.

"Okay, Sig," he called out. "Let's go."

They took the lift to the ground floor, left by way of
the front entrance and hurried to the car.

Its engine was still idling.

Render opened the passenger door and Sigmund leapt
in. He squeezed by him into the driver's seat then, but the
dog was already pushing the primary coordinates and the
address tabs with his paw.

Looks like I'm in the wrong seat.

He lit a cigarette as the car swept ahead into a Uunderpass. It emerged on the opposite marginal, sat poised a moment, then joined the traffic flow. The dog directed the car into the high-acceleration lane.

"Oh," said the dog, "oh."

Render felt like patting his head at that moment, but he looked at him, saw that his teeth were bared, and decided against it.

"When did she start acting peculiar?" he asked.

"Came home from work. Did not eat. Would not answer me, when I talked. Just sits."

"Has she ever been like this before?"

"No."

What could have precipitated it?—but maybe she just had a bad day. After all, he's only a dog—sort of.—No. He'd know. But what, then?

"How was she yesterday—and when she left home this morning?"

"Like always."

Render tried, calling her again. There was still no answer.

"You, did, it," said the dog.

"What do you mean?"

"Eyes. Seeing. You. Machine. Bad."

"No," said Render, and his hand rested on the unit of stunspray in his pocket.

"Yes," said the dog, turning to him again. "You will, make her well . . . ?"

"Of course," said Render.

Sigmund stared ahead again.

Render felt physically exhilarated and mentally sluggish. He sought the confusion factor. He had had these feelings about the case since that first session. There was something very unsettling about Eileen Shallot: a combination of high intelligence and helplessness, of determination and vulnerability, of sensitivity and bitterness.

Do I find that especially attractive?—No. It's just the counter-transference, damn it!

"You smell afraid," said the dog.

"Then color me afraid," said Render, "and turn the page."

They slowed for a series of turns, picked up speed again, slowed again, picked up speed again. Finally, they were traveling along a narrow section of roadway through a semiresidential area of town. The car turned up a side street, proceeded about half a mile further, clicked softly beneath its dashboard, and turned into the parking lot behind a high brick apartment building. The click must have been a special servomech which took over from the point where the monitor released it, because the car crawled across the lot, headed into its transparent parking stall, then stopped. Render turned off the ignition.

Sigmund had already opened the door on his side. Render followed him into the building, and they rode the elevator to the fiftieth floor. The dog dashed on ahead up the hallway, pressed his nose against a plate set low in a doorframe, and waited. After a moment, the door swung several inches inward. He pushed it open with his shoulder and entered. Render followed, closing the door behind him.

The apartment was large, its walls pretty much unadorned, its color combinations unnerving. A great library of tapes filled one corner; a monstrous combination-broadcaster stood beside it. There was a wide bow-legged table set in front of the window, and a low couch along the right hand wall; there was a closed door beside the couch; an archway to the left apparently led to other rooms. Eileen sat in an overstuffed chair in the far corner by the window. Sigmund stood beside the chair.

Render crossed the room and extracted a cigarette from his case. Snapping open his lighter, he held the flame until her head turned in that direction.

"Cigarette?" he asked.

"Charles?"

"Right."

"Yes, thank you. I will."

She held out her hand, accepted the cigarette, put it to her lips.

"Thanks.—What are you doing here?"

"Social call. I happened to be in the neighborhood."

"I didn't hear a buzz, or a knock."

"You must have been dozing. Sig let me in."

"Yes, I must have." She stretched. "What time is it?"

"It's close to four-thirty."

"I've been home over two hours then . . . Must have been very tired . . ."

"How do you feel now?"

"Fine," she declared. "Care for a cup of coffee?"

"Don't mind if I do."

"A steak to go with it?"

"No thanks."

"Bicardi in the coffee?"

"Sounds good."

"Excuse me then. It'll only take a moment."

She went through the door beside the sofa, and Render caught a glimpse of a large, shiny, automatic kitchen.

"Well?" he whispered to the dog.

Sigmund shook his head.

"Not same."

Render shook his head.

He deposited his coat on the sofa, folding it carefully about the medkit. He sat beside it and thought.

Did I throw too big a chunk of seeing at once? Is she suffering from depressive side-effects—say, memory repressions, nervous fatigue? Did I upset her sensory adaptation syndrome somehow? Why have I been proceeding so rapidly anyway? There's no real hurry. Am I so damned eager to write the thing up?—Or am I doing it because she wants me to? Could she be that strong, consciously or unconsciously? Or am I that vulnerable—somehow?

She called him to the kitchen to carry out the tray. He set it on the table and seated himself across from her.

"Good coffee," he said, burning his lips on the cup.

"Smart machine," she stated, facing his voice.

Sigmund stretched out on the carpet next to the table, lowered his head between his forepaws, sighed, and closed his eyes.

"I've been wondering," said Render, "whether or not there were any aftereffects to that last session—like increased synesthesiac experiences, or dreams involving forms, or hallucinations or . . ."

"Yes," she said flatly, "dreams."

"What kind?"

"That last session. I've dreamt it over, and over."

"Beginning to end?"

"No, there's no special order to the events. We're riding through the city, or over the bridge, or sitting at the table, or walking toward the car—just flashes like that. Vivid ones."

"What sort of feelings accompany these—flashes?"

"I don't know. They're all mixed up."

"What are your feelings now, as you recall them."

"The same, all mixed up."

"Are you afraid?"

"N-no. I don't think so."

"Do you want to take a vacation from the thing? Do you feel we've been proceeding too rapidly?"

"No. That's not it at all. It's—well, it's like learning to swim. When you finally learn how, why then you swim and you swim and you swim until you're all exhausted. Then you just lie there gasping in the air and remembering what it was like, while your friends all hover and chew you out for overexerting yourself—and it's a good feeling, even though you do take a chill and there's pins and needles inside all your muscles. At least, that's the way I do things. I felt that way after the first session and after this last one. First Times are always very special times . . . The pins and the needles are gone, though, and I've caught my breath again. Lord, I don't want to stop now! I feel fine."

"Do you usually take a nap in the afternoon?"

The ten red nails of her fingernails moved across the tabletop as she stretched.

". . . Tired." She smiled, swallowing a yawn. "Half the staff's on vacation or sick leave and I've been beating my brains out all week. I was about ready to fall on my face when I left work. I feel all right now that I've rested, though."

She picked up her coffee cup with both hands, took a large swallow.

"Uh-huh," he said. "Good. I was a bit worried about you. I'm glad to see there was no reason."

"Worried? You've read Dr. Riscomb's notes on my analysis—and on the ONT&R trial—and you think I'm the sort to worry about? Ha! I have an operationally beneficient neurosis concerning my adequacy as a human being. It focuses my energies, coordinates my efforts toward achievement. It enhances my sense of identity . . ."

"You do have one hell of a memory," he noted. "That's almost verbatim."

"Of course."

"You had Sigmund worried today, too."

"Sig? How?"

The dog stirred uneasily, opened one eye.

"Yes," he growled, glaring up at Render. "He needs, a ride, home."

"Have you been driving the car again?"

"Yes."

"After I told you not to?"

"Yes."

"Why?"

"I was a, fraid. You would, not, answer me, when I talked."

"I was *very* tired—and if you ever take the car again, I'm going to have the door fixed so you can't come and go as you please."

"Sorry,"

"There's nothing wrong with me."

"I, see."

"You are *never* to do it again."

"Sorry." His eye never left Render; it was like a burning lens.

Render looked away.

"Don't be too hard on the poor fellow," he said. "After all, he thought you were ill and he went for the doctor. Supposing he'd been right? You'd owe him thanks, not a scolding."

Unmollified, Sigmund glared a moment longer and closed his eye.

"He has to be told when he does wrong," she finished.

"I suppose," he said, drinking his coffee. "No harm done, anyhow. Since I'm here, let's talk shop. I'm writing something and I'd like an opinion."

"Great. Give me a footnote?"

"Two or three.—In your opinion, do the general underlying motivations that lead to suicide differ in different cultures?"

"My well-considered opinion is no, they don't," she said. "Frustrations can lead to depressions or frenzies; and if these are severe enough, they can lead to self-destruction. You ask me about motivations and I think they stay pretty much the same. I feel this is a cross-cultural, cross-temporal aspect of the human condition. I don't think it could be changed without changing the basic nature of man."

"Okay. Check. Now, what of the inciting element?" he asked. "Let man be a constant, his environment is still a variable. If he is placed in an overprotective life-situation, do you feel it would take more or less to depress him—or stimulate him to frenzy—than it would take in a not so protective environment?"

"Hm. Being case-oriented, I'd say it would depend on the man. But I see what you're driving at: a mass predisposition to jump out windows at the drop of a hat—the window even opening itself for you, because you asked it to—the revolt of the bored masses. I don't like the notion. I hope it's wrong."

"So do I, but I was thinking of symbolic suicides too—functional disorders that occur for pretty flimsy reasons."

"Aha! Your lecture last month: autopsychomimesis. I have the tape. Well-told, but I can't agree."

"Neither can I, now. I'm rewriting that whole section—

'Thanatos in Cloudcuckooland,' I'm calling it. It's really the death-instinct moved nearer the surface."

"If I get you a scalpel and a cadaver, will you cut out the death-instinct and let me touch it?"

"Couldn't," he put the grin into his voice, "it would be all used up in a cadaver. Find me a volunteer though, and he'll prove my case by volunteering."

"Your logic is unassailable." She smiled. "Get us some more coffee, okay?"

Render went to the kitchen, spiked and filled the cups, drank a glass of water, returned to the living room. Eileen had not moved; neither had Sigmund.

"What do you do when you're not busy being a Shaper?" she asked him.

"The same things most people do—eat, drink, sleep, talk, visit friends, and not-friends, visit places, read . . ."

"Are you a forgiving man?"

"Sometimes. Why?"

"Then forgive me. I argued with a woman today, a woman named DeVille."

"What about?"

"You—she accused me of such things it were better my mother had not born me. Are you going to marry her?"

"No, marriage is like alchemy. It served an important purpose once, but I hardly feel it's here to stay."

"Good."

"What did you say to her?"

"I gave her a clinic referral card that said, 'Diagnosis: Bitch. Prescription: Drug therapy and a tight gag.' "

"Oh," said Render, showing interest.

"She tore it up and threw it in my face."

"I wonder why?"

She shrugged, smiled, made a gridwork on the table-cloth.

" 'Fathers and elders, I ponder,' " sighed Render, " 'what is hell?' "

" 'I maintain it is the suffering of being unable to love,' " she finished. "Was Dostoevsky right?"

"I doubt it. I'd put him into group therapy, myself. That'd be *real* hell for him—with all those people acting like his characters, and enjoying it so."

Render put down his cup, pushed his chair away from the table.

"I suppose you must be going now?"

"I really should," said Render.

"And I can't interest you in food?"

"No."

She stood.

"Okay, I'll get my coat."

"I could drive back myself and just set the car to return."

"No! I'm frightened by the notion of empty cars driving around the city. I'd feel the thing was haunted for the next two-and-a-half weeks.

"Besides," she said, passing through the archway, "you promised me Winchester Cathedral."

"You want to do it today?"

"If you can be persuaded."

As Render stood deciding, Sigmund rose to his feet. He stood directly before him and stared upward into his eyes. He opened his mouth and closed it, several times, but no sounds emerged. Then he turned away and left the room.

"No," Eileen's voice came back, "you will stay here until I return."

Render picked up his coat and put it on, stuffing the medkit into the far pocket.

As they walked up the hall toward the elevator, Render thought he heard a very faint and very distant howling sound.

In this place, of all places, Render knew he was the master of all things.

He was at home on those alien worlds, without time, those worlds where flowers copulate and the stars do battle in the heavens, falling at last to the ground, bleeding, like so many split and shattered chalices, and the seas part to reveal stairways leading down, and arms emerge from caverns, waving torches that flame like liquid faces —a midwinter night's nightmare, summer go a-begging, Render knew—for he had visited those worlds on a professional basis for the better part of a decade. With the crooking of a finger he could isolate the sorcerers, bring them to trial for treason against the realm—aye, and he could execute them, could appoint their successors.

Fortunately, this trip was only a courtesy call . . .

He moved forward through the glade, seeking her.

He could feel her awakening presence all about him.

He pushed through the branches, stood beside the lake. It was cold, blue, and bottomless, the lake, reflecting that slender willow which had become the station of her arrival.

"Eileen!"

The willow swayed toward him, swayed away.

"Eileen! Come forth!"

Leaves fell, floated upon the lake, disturbed its mirror-like placidity, distorted the reflections.

"Eileen?"

All the leaves yellowed at once then, dropped down into the water. The tree ceased its swaying. There was a strange sound in the darkening sky, like the humming of high wires on a cold day.

Suddenly there was a double file of moons passing through the heavens.

Render selected one, reached up and pressed it. The others vanished as he did so, and the world brightened; the humming went out of the air.

He circled the lake to gain a subjective respite from the rejection-action and his counter to it. He moved up along an aisle of pines toward the place where he wanted the cathedral to occur. Birds sang now in the trees. The wind came softly by him. He felt her presence quite strongly.

"Here, Eileen. Here."

She walked beside him then, green silk, hair of bronze, eyes of molten emerald; she wore an emerald in her fore-head. She walked in green slippers over the pine needles, saying: "What happened?"

"You were afraid."

"Why?"

"Perhaps you fear the cathedral. Are you a witch?" He smiled.

"Yes, but it's my day off'."

He laughed, and he took her arm, and they rounded an island of foliage, and there was the cathedral recon-structed on a grassy rise, pushing its way above them and above the trees, climbing into the middle air, breath-ing out organ notes, reflecting a stray ray of sunlight from a plane of glass.

"Hold tight to the world," he said. "Here comes the guided tour."

They moved forward and entered.

" '. . . With its floor-to-ceiling shafts, like so many huge treetrunks, it achieves a ruthless control over its spaces,' " he said. "—Got that from the guidebook. This is the north transept . . ."

" 'Greensleeves,' " she said, "the organ is playing 'Greensleeves.' "

"So it is. You can't blame me for that though.—Observe the scalloped capitals—"

"I want to go nearer the music."

"Very well. This way then."

Render felt that something was wrong. He could not put his finger on it.

Everything retained its solidity . . .

Something passed rapidly then, high above the cathedral, uttering a sonic boom. Render smiled at that, remembering now; it was like a slip of the tongue: for a moment he had confused Eileen with Jill—yes, that was what had happened.

Why, then . . .

A burst of white was the altar. He had never seen it before, anywhere. All the walls were dark and cold about them. Candles flickered in corners and high niches. The organ chorded thunder under invisible hands.

Render knew that something was wrong.

He turned to Eileen Shallot, whose hat was a green cone towering up into the darkness, trailing wisps of green veiling. Her throat was in shadow, but . . .

"That necklace—Where?"

"I don't know." She smiled.

The goblet she held radiated a rosy light. It was reflected from her emerald. It washed him like a draft of cool air.

"Drink?" she asked.

"Stand still," he ordered.

He willed the walls to fall down. They swam in shadow.

"Stand still!" he repeated urgently. "Don't do anything. Try not even to think.

"—Fall down!" he cried. And the walls were blasted in all directions and the roof was flung over the top of the world, and they stood amid ruins lighted by a single taper. The night was black as pitch.

"Why did you do that?" she asked, still holding the goblet out toward him.

"Don't think. Don't think anything," he said. "Relax. You are very tired. As that candle flickers and wanes so does your consciousness. You can barely keep awake. You can hardly stay on your feet. Your eyes are closing. There is nothing to see here anyway."

He willed the candle to go out. It continued to burn.

"I'm not tired. Please have a drink."

He heard organ music through the night. A different tune, one he did not recognize at first.

"I need your cooperation."

"All right. Anything."

"Look! The moon!" He pointed.

She looked upward and the moon appeared from behind an inky cloud.

". . . And another, and another."

Moons, like strung pearls, proceeded across the blackness.

"The last one will be red," he stated.

It was.

He reached out then with his right index finger, slid his arm sideways along his field of vision, then tried to touch the red moon.

His arm ached; it burned. He could not move it.

"Wake up!" he screamed.

The red moon vanished, and the white ones.

"Please take a drink."

He dashed the goblet from her hand and turned away. When he turned back she was still holding it before him.

"A drink?"

He turned and fled into the night.

It was like running through a waist-high snowdrift. It was wrong. He was compounding the error by running—he was minimizing his strength, maximizing hers. It was sapping his energies, draining him.

He stood still in the midst of the blackness.

"The world around me moves," he said. "I am its center."

"Please have a drink," she said, and he was standing in the glade beside their table set beside the lake. The lake was black and the moon was silver, and high, and out of his reach. A single candle flickered on the table, making her hair as silver as her dress. She wore the moon on her brow. A bottle of Romanee-Conti stood on the white cloth beside a wide-brimmed wine glass. It was filled to overflowing, that glass, and rosy beads clung to its lip. He was very thirsty, and she was lovelier than anyone he had ever seen before, and her necklace sparkled, and the breeze came cool off the lake, and there was something—something he should remember . . .

He took a step toward her and his armor clinked lightly as he moved. He reached toward the glass and his right arm stiffened with pain and fell back to his side.

"You are wounded!"

Slowly, he turned his head. The blood flowed from the open wound in his bicep and ran down his arm and dripped from his fingertips. His armor had been breached. He forced himself to look away.

"Drink this, love. It will heal you."

She stood.

"I will hold the glass."

He stared at her as she raised it to his lips.

"Who am I?" he asked.

She did not answer him, but something replied—within a splashing of waters out over the lake:

"You are Render, the Shaper."

"Yes, I remember," he said; and turning his mind to the one lie which might break the entire illusion he forced his mouth to say: "Eileen Shallot, I hate you."

The world shuddered and swam about him, was shaken, as by a huge sob.

"Charles!" she screamed, and the blackness swept over them.

"Wake up! Wake up!" he cried, and his right arm burned and ached and bled in the darkness.

He stood alone in the midst of a white plain. It was silent, it was endless. It sloped away toward the edges of the world. It gave off its own light, and the sky was no sky, but was nothing overhead. Nothing. He was alone. His own voice echoed back to him from the end of the world: ". . . hate you," it said, ". . . hate you."

He dropped to his knees. He was Render.

He wanted to cry.

A red moon appeared above the plain, casting a ghastly light over the entire expanse. There was a wall of mountains to the left of him, another to his right.

He raised his right arm. He helped it with his left hand. He clutched his wrist, extended his index finger. He reached for the moon.

Then there came a howl from high in the mountains, a great wailing cry—half-human, all challenge, all loneliness and all remorse. He saw it then, treading upon the

176

mountains, its tail brushing the snow from their highest peaks, the ultimate loupgarou of the North—Fenris, son of Loki—raging at the heavens.

It leapt into the air. It swallowed the moon.

It landed near him, and its great eyes blazed yellow. It stalked him on soundless pads, across the cold white fields that lay between the mountains; and he backed away from it, up hills and down slopes, over crevasses and rifts, through valleys, past stalagmites and pinnacles —under the edges of glaciers, beside frozen riverbeds, and always downwards—until its hot breath bathed him and its laughing mouth was opened above him.

He turned then and his feet became two gleaming rivers carrying him away.

The world jumped backwards. He glided over the slopes. Downward. Speeding—

Away . . .

He looked back over his shoulder.

In the distance, the gray shape loped after him.

He felt that it could narrow the gap if it chose. He had to move faster.

The world reeled about him. Snow began to fall.

He raced on. Ahead, a blur, a broken outline.

He tore through the veils of snow which now seemed to be falling upward from off the ground—like strings of bubbles.

He approached the shattered form.

Like a swimmer he approached—unable to open his mouth to speak, for fear of drowning—of drowning and not knowing, of never knowing.

He could not check his forward motion; he was swept tidelike toward the wreck. He came to a stop, at last, before it.

Some things never change. They are things which have long ceased to exist as objects and stand solely as never-to-be-calendared occasions outside that sequence of elements called Time.

Render stood there and did not care if Fenris leapt upon his back and ate his brains. He had covered his eyes, but he could not stop the seeing. Not this time. He did not care about anything. Most of himself lay dead at his feet.

There was a howl. A gray shape swept past him.

The baleful eyes and bloody muzzle rooted within the wrecked car, champing through the steel, the glass, groping inside for . . .

"No! Brute! Chewer of corpses!" he cried. "The dead are sacred! *My* dead are sacred!"

He had a scalpel in his hand then, and he slashed expertly at the tendons, the bunches of muscle on the straining shoulders, the soft belly, the ropes of the arteries.

Weeping, he dismembered the monster, limb by limb, and it bled and it bled, fouling the vehicle and remains within it with its infernal animal juices, dripping and running until the whole plain was reddened and writhing about them.

Render fell across the pulverized hood, and it was soft and warm and dry. He wept upon it.

"Don't cry," she said.

He was hanging onto her shoulder then, holding her tightly, there beside the black lake beneath the moon that was Wedgewood. A single candle flickered upon their table. She held the glass to his lips.

"Please drink it."

"Yes, give it to me!"

He gulped the wine that was all softness and lightness. It burned within him. He felt his strength returning.

"I am . . ."

"—*Render, the Shaper,*" splashed the lake.

"No!"

He turned and ran again, looking for the wreck. He had to go back, to return . . .

"You can't."

"I can!" he cried. "I can, if I try . . ."

Yellow flames coiled through the thick air. Yellow serpents. They coiled, glowing, about his ankles. Then through the murk, two-headed and towering, approached his Adversary.

Small stones rattled past him. An overpowering odor corkscrewed up his nose and into his head.

"Shaper!" came the bellow from one head.

"You have returned for the reckoning!" called the other.

Render stared, remembering.

"No reckoning, Thaumiel," he said. "I beat you and I chained you for—Rothman, yes it was Rothman—the cabalist." He traced a pentagram in the air. "Return to Qliphoth. I banish you."

"This place be Qliphoth."

". . . By Khamael, the angel of blood, by the hosts of Seraphim, in the Name of Elohim Gebor, I bid you vanish!"

"Not this time." Both heads laughed.

It advanced.

Render backed slowly away, his feet bound by the yellow serpents. He could feel the chasm opening behind him. The world was a jigsaw puzzle coming apart. He could see the pieces separating.

"Vanish!"

The giant roared out its double-laugh.

Render stumbled.

"This way, love!"

She stood within a small cave to his right.

He shook his head and backed toward the chasm.

Thaumiel reached out toward him.

Render toppled back over the edge.

"Charles!" she screamed, and the world shook itself apart with her wailing.

"Then Vernichtung," he answered as he fell. "I join you in darkness."

Everything came to an end.

"I want to see Dr. Charles Render."

"I'm sorry, that is impossible."

"But I skip-jetted all the way here, just to thank him. I'm a new man! He changed my life!"

"I'm sorry, Mister Erikson. When you called this morning, I told you it was impossible."

"Sir, I'm Representative Erikson—and Render once did me a great service."

"Then you can do him one now. Go home."

"You can't talk to me that way!"

"I just did. Please leave. Maybe next year sometime . . ."

"But a few words can do wonders . . ."

"Save them!"

"I—I'm sorry . . ."

Lovely as it was, pinked over with the morning—the slopping, steaming bowl of the sea—he knew that it *had* to end. Therefore . . .

He descended the high tower stairway and he entered the courtyard. He crossed to the bower of roses and he looked down upon the pallet set in its midst.

"Good morrow, m'lord," he said.

"To you the same," said the knight, his blood mingling with the earth, the flowers, the grasses, flowing from his wound, sparkling over his armor, dripping from his fingertips.

"Naught hath healed?"

The knight shook his head.

"I empty. I wait."

"Your waiting is near ended."

"What mean you?" he sat upright.

"The ship. It approacheth harbor."

The knight stood. He leaned his back against a mossy treetrunk. He stared at the huge, bearded servitor who continued to speak, words harsh with barbaric accents:

"It cometh like a dark swan before the wind—returning."

"Dark, say you? Dark?"

"The sails be black, Lord Tristram."

"You lie!"

"Do you wish to see? To see for yourself?—Look then!"

He gestured.

The earth quaked, the wall toppled. The dust swirled and settled. From where they stood they could see the ship moving into the harbor on the wings of the night.

"No! You lied!—See! They are white!"

The dawn danced upon the waters. The shadows fled from the ship's sails.

"No, you fool! Black! They *must* be!"

"White! White!—Ksolde! You have kept faith! You have returned!"

He began running toward the harbor.

"Come back!—Your wound! You are ill!—Stop . . ."

The sails were white beneath a sun that was a red button which the servitor reached quickly to touch.

Night fell.

A thrilling novel of near future catastrophe!

With the excitement of *The Andromeda Strain* and the sophistication of *Lucifer's Hammer*, SKYFALL is a thrilling novel of near future catastrophe—a catastrophe with a chilling ring of authenticity in the wake of this year's nuclear satellite fall in Canada....

SPECIAL:
SKYFALL will feature two striking covers—one depicting a science fiction theme, the other, the "disaster" novel look. They'll both catch your eye so be on the lookout for them!

PROJECT PROMETHEUS WOULD STEAL THE FIRE OF THE SUN—
BUT THE PRICE MIGHT BE TOO TERRIBLE TO CONTEMPLATE

A NOVEL OF THE NEAR FUTURE BY
HARRY HARRISON

SKYFALL

$1.95

ACE
SCIENCE
FICTION

360 PARK AVENUE SOUTH · NEW YORK, N.Y. 10010

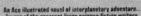

105

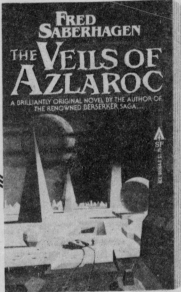

A novel of cosmic adventure from the author of PATTERNS OF CHAOS!

$1⁹⁵

Only men already under sentence of death are offered the chance to become Ion warriors—no one else would be willing to endure the agony of Ion transformation!

An Ace Science Fiction Original Novel

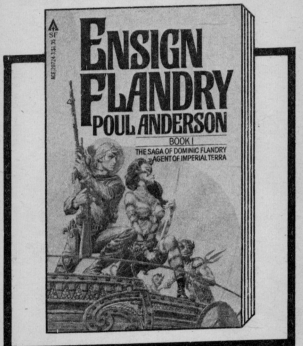

Zero Population Growth Achieved!

But at what cost? The world now exists with a mandatory abortion law and sexual freedom reigns. Is this truly a world where... **LOVE CONQUERS ALL**

$1.95